WILL JANET EVER LEARN THE SECRET OF HER FATHER'S DEATH?

Janet Vance is convinced that her Uncle Lew was murdered just as he was about to discover the secret behind her father's strange death. She must uncover the mystery shrouding both their deaths in order to clear the family name.

But someone—or something—is trying to stop her. From the moment she finds a letter in an old roll top desk in the house she inherited from her uncle, strange, unexplainable things begin to happen.

Voice On The Wind

Dorothy Daniels

PAPERBACK LIBRARY

New York

PAPERBACK LIBRARY EDITION
First Printing: May, 1969

*Paperback Library is a division of Coronet Communications,
Inc. Its trademark, consisting of the words "Paperback Library"
accompanied by an open book, is registered in the United States
Patent Office. Coronet Communications, Inc., 315 Park Avenue
South, New York, N.Y. 10010.*

ONE

Each time I think back on that ill-fated occasion, three sounds are still impressed on my mind. Nor do they seem to fade with the passage of time for even now I shudder whenever I recall the tolling of the buoy bells in the harbor, the wail of foghorns on the rocks, the clop-clop of the horse's hoofs on the cobblestones as it pulled the coach in which my aunt and I were riding, plus those of the four back-plumed horses drawing the hearse directly ahead.

The day was as melancholy as the event was mournful. The fog, which had been in evidence for a week now, was a thick gray curtain outside the windows of the coach. There was a stillness all about us, except for the sounds which I mentioned.

I was dressed appropriately in black, with a small toque atop my head. I'd draped it with a mourning veil which I'd purchased two years before, except that then no hearse rode before the carriage, for it was a memorial service for my father, and, at that time, the only other occupant of the coach was my Uncle Lew. Now I was on my way to attend funeral services for him. Seated opposite me today was Nancy Vance, the wife—or rather widow—of my uncle.

Nan was fifty, angular, crochety, stern-faced and unyielding. She was dressed in proper mourning also, with her veil thrown back so that she might touch her eyes now and then with a black-bordered handkerchief, though I saw no evidence of tears.

"How could he have done such a thing?" she said morosely, more to herself than me. "To think of it . . .

5

drunk and undoubtedly disorderly . . . shaming me, even in the manner of his death."

"Stop it, Aunt Nancy!" I said, my tone as severe as I could make it. "We're on our way to attend the funeral rites of your husband. Kindly make the effort to show that your grief is for him rather than for yourself."

"How dare you speak to me in this fashion!" she retorted, regarding me with open distaste. "It is your father who first brought disgrace on this family."

"The story regarding my father is disgraceful, I will admit," I replied. "However, I do not believe a word of it. Neither do I believe my uncle was inebriated at the time of his death."

"I suppose you will even deny he drank," she retorted caustically.

"This is not the time for such talk, Auntie," I said patiently. "I wish to pay the proper respect to my uncle. We are his only mourners."

"What do you expect? He disgraced himself before the whole town. How grateful I am that there is this heavy fog which conceals us from the eyes of the townfolk."

"Are you such a coward?" I asked incredulously. "Thank goodness my uncle wasn't. From the time Papa's ship went down, Uncle Lew spent his days trying to learn the truth of what really happened."

"We know the truth," my aunt replied sternly. "Your father was drunk also. He betrayed his passengers. They're all dead because of him."

"I'll never believe it," I said quietly.

"I believe it," she said angrily.

"Please, Auntie," I pleaded. "Let's not quarrel. You've never spoken to me with such bitterness before."

"Not because I didn't wish to. It was your uncle who made me hold my tongue. But there's no further need to—any more than there is any further need for you to call me auntie. When the services are over, you will leave my home."

"Be assured I will. In the meantime, should I address you as Mrs. Vance?"

"Nancy will do," she replied. "You'll be here such a little while, it won't matter."

The horse drawing the coach slowed and stopped. It was impossible to see the church through the fog, but we knew we had arrived. The driver opened the door and assisted my aunt and me from the coach. Standing beside the hearse were four ne'er-do-wells who practically lived at the tavern. I'd paid them well to come here and carry the casket of my uncle into the church.

It was a tragic thing to behold, for the name of Vance had stood for all that was brave and courageous in this town from 1859 until the year of 1893 when my father had allegedly tarnished the name. Now, in 1895, my uncle had completed the disgrace with his tragic death. At least, that's what the town believed and openly stated.

Not a single occupant of the town was in sight. My heart ached at sight of the empty pews. We followed the men carrying the casket to the front of the church. When it was set down, we took our place in the pew.

The minister seemed properly sympathetic, and his obsequy mercifully brief. There was no organ music. The only wreath was the sheaf of field daisies which I'd picked this morning. They lay on the closed casket, looking as forlorn as the day and the occasion.

I was grateful for the town ne'er-do-wells who stood at attention on either side of the casket during the ceremony which took no more than ten minutes. I suppose that my uncle had, on occasion, bought them drinks. At least they were doing their best to earn their money. I supposed too that near the end of his life they were the only ones who would talk with him. I knew he'd brooded not so much on the death of my father as the scandal caused by the death. Papa had been accused of a most unforgivable sin. Now my uncle had been accused of tippling to the extent he had fallen over the high cliff. I not only could not, I would not believe such a tale. My uncle was not a drunkard. He drank, yes, but not to the extent that his steps faltered, his mind became befuddled. He was not a fool; he knew that bluff as well as I. If he'd over-indulged in alcoholic spirits, he'd never have gone near that dangerous precipice.

I heard the shuffling of steps as someone prepared to leave the church and I looked around. Much to my surprise there were two gentlemen at the rear. One, middle-aged, occupied a pew on one side. The other, young, sat on the opposite side.

The young gentleman was tall, slender, with a thick mop of unruly reddish-brown hair. He had a craggy sort of face and, even at this distance, I could see he was studying me intently, as if his eyes were trying to pierce the opaqueness of the mourning veil.

I turned my attention back to the service. The four hired pallbearers picked up the casket and moved down the aisle with it. We followed the minister to the graveyard beside the church. The grave was already prepared, the coffin about to be lowered—too quickly, I thought. As if the few connected with the ceremony wanted to get it over with.

The minister scooped up a handful of earth and dropped it onto the casket, intoning his mournful words. Then it was over. On our way back to the coach, I cast a few furtive glances about to see if either gentleman was evident. It was difficult to see more than a few feet because of the fog, but if they had come to see my uncle's remains lowered into the earth, there was no sign of them. I wondered who they were and what had prompted them to come.

My aunt and I maintained a discreet silence on our way back to the large house atop the bluff. I wondered what she was thinking. As for myself, my heart suddenly felt overwhelmed with grief as the realization came that I would never see Uncle Lew again. He'd been very kind to me. I knew, in his way, that he'd loved me and had done everything possible to make me happy. I also knew now that his wife had merely tolerated me.

Papa had brought me to their home when Mama died. Up until her death, the three of us traveled the seas. She tutored me and once each year I was taken to New York for examinations in the private school which set up and mailed studies for me to do each year. I'd had a full life up until Mama's death, for the ports all over the world were my doorstep.

Three years ago, while we were at sea, Mama had been taken ill with a violent fever and died. She was buried at sea, which was what she and Papa had both always wanted, for they loved the water, whether it was tranquil or angry. And they had taught me to love it also.

After her death, Papa brought me to live with Uncle Lew and his wife. Papa's tragic death at sea followed Mama's by one year.

Now I was alone, and there wasn't another soul in this world who cared about my presence. I'd leave this village as soon as possible. At the same time, I wanted to stay—to prove the villagers wrong, both as to my uncle and my father. Yet how could I? And where would I start? The very thought was ridiculous. Certainly my aunt would not tolerate me in her home any longer than was necessary. By the same token, I wasn't relishing her company. The quicker I got away from here, the better off I would be. Only then, would my life begin anew.

Though I had not been trained for work, I felt my education would stand me in good stead. I could hire out as a tutor, or perhaps even as a teacher in some rural location. I prayed it would be near the water. I couldn't bear the thought of living away from the sea—perhaps because it had claimed the remains of both my parents. Whatever the reason, the sea always seemed more my home than any house.

Once again the coach stopped and we knew we had reached the house. It was a splendid abode, three stories high, with a widow's walk atop. There were four double chimneys jutting from its roof, for there were eight large rooms in the house and each had its own fireplace. The edifice had a strong, courageous look, as if defying anything the Atlantic could hurl at it in the form of sleet, snow, rain or wind.

I paid the driver, then moved into step with Nancy. I no longer thought of her as my aunt, since it was her wish I not do so.

"Do you suppose his spirit is in the house?" she asked, almost fearfully, I thought.

"I don't believe in spirits or ghouls or haunts," I replied quietly. I almost added that only the ignorant and uneducated believed in such nonsense, but I thought in time. I didn't want any further cruel or unkind words to be exchanged. Though I knew she'd never felt any affection

9

for me, neither had I ever seen her display any for my uncle. It was her way and I had come to accept it. Now, of course, I was aware of her dislike for me.

"You're a very haughty person," she said.

"I don't mean to be," I said thoughtfully. "I traveled about a great deal with Mama and Papa. They allowed me to express my thoughts freely. They encouraged me to think and even more, to listen. In that way, I acquired knowledge and I developed confidence. I think that is one of the reasons Uncle Lew enjoyed talking with me as if I were mature beyond my years."

"Indeed," she said, looking bored. "How soon will you be leaving?"

"As soon as possible," I said.

"Tomorrow," she said, making it a statement, rather than a question.

"If that is what you wish, yes," I replied.

She entered the house and I started to follow but as quickly paused, for just then a shaft of sunlight cut through the fog and revealed the hosts of flowers lining the walk. Though it was still early summer, the season had been unusually warm and the marigolds, nasturtiums, pinks and ragged ladies made a lovely path to the door.

In the fields along the bluff, the bayberries, pokeberries, false lilies of the valley, and daisies provided color even under this blanket of fog, which seemed thicker here, near the edge of the bluff. The sound of the surf seemed to come from a great distance, measured by the toll of the bell buoys.

I stepped into a long hallway, sparsely furnished up to the foot of the staircase, where two granite busts rested on pedestals, and paintings were affixed to the wall so that each had its own step to look down upon. They were my mother's work, done up to the time of her death.

Off the hallway downstairs were three rooms. The parlor was unusually large, being the only room on that side of the house. The carpet was gray with an oval-shaped hooked rug atop it. The furniture was haircloth and walnut, heavy and traditional. All tables were marble-topped and each supported a Victorian lamp. There was a mirror above the great fireplace, and reflected in it were

10

several silver-coated vases which sat on the mantel. It was a restful room, if not one of the most cheerful I had ever seen.

Nancy removed her hat and veil, placed them carefully on one of the tables. Then she sat down primly in a chair near the window.

"Do you wish the fireplace lit?" I asked, removing my own hat and veil.

"Yes," she replied tersely. "We shall have a guest presently."

I immediately thought of the young man I'd seen in the church and my brows raised questioningly. Apparently Nancy noticed.

"Not the young stranger who was in the church," she said, as if reading my mind.

"Do you know him?" I asked foolishly.

"Would I call him a stranger if I did?" she asked sensibly.

"There were two gentlemen in the church," I replied.

"I know that and it's the older one I'm referring to," she said. "His name is Mr. LeMay Fillmore."

I suddenly remembered Uncle Lew mentioning the name. I lit the fire and stood before it, watching it come to life and welcoming its warmth.

"He's your uncle's attorney," she informed me. "I suppose I should say he's mine since your uncle's dead."

"Uncle Lew told me once he had a copy of the will here," I said. "He even told me where it was."

"Indeed," she said. "Mr. Fillmore will be here shortly. I sent a telegraph as soon as your uncle's body was found."

"Why don't you refer to Uncle Lew as your husband?" I asked, unable to hide the pique I felt at her coldness.

"He *is* your uncle, isn't he?"

"Yes," I admitted. "He's also your husband."

"He was my husband," she retorted. "He's dead now."

"Did you ever love him?" My tone was as hostile as hers.

"How impertinent you are," she said caustically. "How careful you were not to let your uncle see the ugly side of you."

11

"Please, let's not quarrel," I said, suddenly contrite, embarrassed at my brazen behavior.

At the same time, I realized how lonely my uncle must have been. Small wonder he'd taken an occasional drink of rum. I knew, no matter what my aunt said, that my uncle was not a drunkard. I knew he went to the tavern, but I'd never once seen him under the influence of alcholic spirits.

He'd been deeply affected by the tragedy which had befallen my father. He'd also become embittered by the attitude of the townspeople, for condemning my father who'd never had the opportunity to defend himself.

My father had gone down with his ship, and passengers and crew had drowned. The word was that he'd been intoxicated. I knew my father had never touched a drop of spirits in his life. He had said many times in my presence that he had a great responsibility in his hands—the lives of others—and he would never do anything to endanger those lives. He kept spirits on board and would serve them to male guests who might come aboard for brief visits while in port, but he always settled for a glass of water.

As for my uncle, he was not a teetotaler, but neither was he a drunkard. Yet when he'd had a fatal fall off the bluff, the word from the medical examiner was that he had been intoxicated because the smell of alcohol was on his breath and on his clothes.

My uncle was a retired sea captain. The word quickly passed through the town that he was no better than his brother—drunkards, both of them. None came to offer my aunt sympathy. I know she was greatly embittered because of it. Not that her sorrow was directed toward her husband, but rather she was filled with self-pity. To me, it seemed a form of poetic justice, for she had refused to come with my uncle and me to the memorial services for my father to the church which we had just left. At that time, there had been but two mourners also, my uncle and me.

I thought of the will which Uncle Lew had pointed out to me. It was kept in one of the upstairs rooms which he had used as a den. The room occupied the entire third floor directly below the widow's walk. The heavy envelope lay in the top drawer of the massive oak rolltop desk. Uncle Lew had shown the envelope to me and told me that I was to get it and bring it to my aunt should anything happen to him. He also told me a copy was in the hands of his lawyer in Kennebunk. The village had no attorney. One would have starved here.

I wished I could go up to his den and sit in his large leather chair, or even use the ladder to reach the high balcony which constituted the widow's walk. I wanted to go there once more before I left this house. I wanted to look at the sea I loved and breathe deeply of its salty air.

"When did your uncle tell you he had a copy of the will in this house?" Nancy asked, breaking into my thoughts.

"About a month ago," I said, turning to her, letting the now-crackling fire warm my back.

"I presume you know where it is," she said, still feeling me out.

"Yes," I replied. I was thoroughly warmed now and moved over to take a chair opposite her. "It's in the top drawer of his rolltop desk."

"Suppose you get it," she said.

"Certainly." I arose and headed for the stairs.

I carried the envelope downstairs with the feeling that this would be one of the last times I'd make this journey. Nancy had moved to a chair closer to the fire.

I handed her the envelope, but she made a deprecatory motion.

"I have a headache," she said. "Read it to me."

"Don't you think we should wait for Mr. Fillmore since he has made the trip here?" I asked.

"I think you should obey me, so long as you are in this house," she replied tersely.

I slit the seal of the outer envope, opened the inner one and took out a single sheet of paper, one side of which was half covered by Uncle Lew's Dicksonian script. I began to read.

"My mind is clear, my body is hale and hearty. I make this will without consulting anyone. To my wife, I leave all my money and investments. There is sufficient to care for her the rest of her life. To my beloved niece Janet Vance, I bequeath all of my personal possessions, the entire contents of my home and the house and property without exception. Knowing my dear wife as I do, I stipulate that should she take any sort of action to recover what I have bequeathed to Janet, then the provision in this document granting her moneys and investments shall be declared invalid and everything I own will become the property of my niece. To Janet, I say again, I do not believe the stories told about the death of my brother and your father. Some day the truth will come out. If not in my lifetime, then in yours, God willing."

It was signed and witnessed by three people of the village.

"Well," Nan gasped, her face livid with anger. "That is the most . . . most degrading document that has ever been read to me. Janet, I accuse you of exerting undue influence upon my late husband to get possession of the house. I do not intend to sit by quietly and let this come to pass!"

For some reason, I felt my spirits lift. My remaining here might help me learn, in some way, the truth of my uncle's tragic and mysterious death. As for my father's death, I had small reason to hope for any success. No one had even the faintest idea of where the ship had gone down.

Yet, now that I knew this house was mine, I was more determined than ever not to say anything that would further my aunt's antagonism toward me. So I knew I must do my best to quietly reason with her.

"Don't do anything foolish, Nancy," I said. "I'll stay out of your way as much as possible. According to the will, I don't see how you can take this house away from me. However, you said Mr. Fillmore would be here shortly. Suppose you discuss the matter with him. He could certainly advise you as to the legality of such a thing."

"But why should you get this house?" she demanded, her eyes sending their message of hatred toward me.

14

"Truly, I don't know," I said. "But since I have it, I'm going to hold onto it—at least for the present."

"What do you mean, for the present?"

I thought for a moment. "I believe Uncle Lew had a reason for leaving this house to me."

"In heaven's name, why?"

"I can't answer that. Or perhaps I can. It may well be he thinks I can clear up the mystery of my father's death. In doing so, perhaps I can clear up the mystery of Uncle Lew's. Goodness knows, it hasn't been easy living in this town, with the scorn and contempt of its inhabitants directed toward me."

"Then why don't you get out?" she screamed. "Your father was no good. Everyone in town knows it. I know it."

"No!" I cried. "I shall not leave. The more diatribe you heap on my father's name, the more determined I am to remain here."

"Then stay." Nancy arose, regarded me scornfully. "I shall pack my things and leave."

"As you wish," I replied, too tired to argue. "But remember, it is not my desire to drive you from this house. Perhaps, one day, I may even give it back to you."

"I cannot understand why my husband neglected to provide for me." Her manner was almost childlike.

"Nancy," I replied chidingly, "you have all the money you will ever require. More than enough. Uncle Lew made some very wise investments. He told me about them."

"He told you quite a lot, didn't he?" she said resentfully.

"Yes," I admitted. "He had to talk to someone. He was a very lonely man."

"All he wanted to talk about was his brother," Nancy said, her voice rising. "I was sick unto death of hearing about it. So were the villagers."

"All Uncle Lew wanted to do was clear his brother's name," I replied, rising. "There is no need for us to go on like this."

"I shall go upstairs and pack," Nancy said, turning to leave the room.

"Should Mr. Fillmore come, may I summon you?"

15

"You may not," she replied. "Just ask him if there's any way I can get this house back."

"I will ask him," I replied. "But whatever he tells me, and whatever he says, I will urge him to write you so you will know I have given you a truthful answer."

"As you wish," came the reply from the hallway. I heard her climb the stairs heavily.

I sat quietly a few minutes longer, scanning the brief will again, wondering what Uncle Lew had on his mind when he wrote it. The answer had to lie somewhere in the past and my mind went back to it.

My father had been Eli Vance, captain of merchant ships sailing the world. Two months prior to his death, he had taken on the assignment of skippering an ocean-going steam yacht owned by Cyrus Plant, one of the wealthiest men in the United States. The yacht was to sail to Morocco where the ceremony of crowning the new king of a small country was drawing society from all over the world.

The ship could sleep thirty persons besides its crew. Twenty men and women, prominent and wealthy, were the passengers, guests of Mr. Plant. The voyage east had been pleasant and successful.

The passengers had attended the formal ceremony at the palace. My father had been there too and wrote home about it in the last letter I ever received from him. He'd described the glitter and pomp, the incredible jewels of the court, and those of the guests, particularly those from the ship he'd captained.

The return journey was apparently equally serene. At one port of call, everyone seemed happy. All passengers, including the owner and his wife, were going directly to an island resort off the coast, some twenty-five miles north of our village so that my father would be practically home when he dropped anchor.

Then that fatal night when the wireless message was received stating that the captain and crew were drunk and mutinous, that the ship was afire and there was no one to control it. Whoever sent the message also said that the ship was going down, crew and passengers were battling for the lifeboats. The message had ended abruptly, without the sender giving any indication as to the location of the ship. It was never heard from again. Some of the wealthiest families in the nation had gone down with it. The news had been a sensation.

There'd been an official inquiry, but as the board had nothing to go on, the investigation was left open in case there might be a survivor. Two years had gone by now and none had appeared, so the likelihood of there being anyone alive to tell what really happened grew more and more remote.

The village had reacted to all the publicity given the scandal. The village had been, since the first cabin was built, a seacoast town dependent on the sea for a living. Therefore any man granted the high position of captain who violated that trust was in immediate disgrace. This was what happened to the memory of my father and in such a vicious manner that I considered it a blessing Mama had not been alive when the tragedy occurred.

Uncle Lew had not believed it, but he'd been as handicapped in getting at the truth as the members of the official inquiry. The location of where the ship had gone down wasn't even known.

Now my uncle was dead, likewise accused of having been drunk. It was deduced he had wandered too close to the edge of the bluff behind the house, lost his footing and plunged to the rocks below. That high, black, awesome bluff—which my uncle had loved and was completely familiar with. In fact, it was his familiarity with the area that caused the villagers to accuse him of drunkenness. They said had he been sober he would never have gone over. I argued that had he been inebriated, he'd never have gone near it; he was far too intelligent. But in the eyes of the villagers I carried the burden of my father's guilt, and nothing I said was given any consideration.

One part of my mind argued it was foolish to remain here. That I'd never know happiness; only scorn and contempt. The other part argued that I had a duty to remain here; for nowhere else would I learn the truth.

The door knocker sounded, interrupting my musings. I hastened to answer the summons and was relieved to see it was the gentleman who had been at the church.

"I'm Mr. LeMay Fillmore," he introduced himself. "I
17

received a telegram from Mrs. Vance informing me her husband had met with an unfortunate accident."

"Please come in, Mr. Fillmore." I opened the door wider. "I'm Janet Vance."

"Ah." He bowed in acknowledgement. "You're Eli Vance's daughter. I'm happy to meet you, Miss Janet."

"Thank you, sir," I said, pleased at his friendliness. I continued to speak as I led the way into the parlor. "I'm honored to meet you. My uncle spoke of you, of course. Thank you for paying your respects at the church."

"He was a fine gentleman," Mr. Fillmore said.

"Yes, he was," I said, motioning him to a chair before the fireplace and seating myself opposite. "Do you know the circumstances of his death?"

"I know only what I've been told in the village," he said. "I don't believe a word of it."

"Thank you, sir," I said. "My uncle did take an occasional drink, but he was not a drunkard. I'm sorely puzzled by his death."

"It's been termed accidental, I know," Mr. Fillmore said.

"I don't believe it," I said, with a firmness that surprised even me.

He regarded me with surprise. "Accidents do happen, you know, Miss Vance."

"True," I acknowledged. "But my uncle was not a stupid man. If he had overindulged—which I never knew of him to do—he would have avoided the bluff. It's a treacherous place even when one has full control of one's senses."

"It is indeed," Mr. Fillmore admitted. "That's what delayed my coming here. I took a look at it."

"That was a very dangerous thing to do with such a heavy fog."

"I agree, but I was most cautious." He looked around him and I knew he questioned my aunt's absence. "Do you suppose Mrs. Vance would see me today? There's a train at five o'clock—it's making a special stop for me. I have a carriage waiting outside to take me to the depot."

My smile was apologetic. "She said she would not be down."

18

"I'm sorry. As you know, I came to read her husband's will."

"She's already familiar with its contents." I reached over and picked up the open will which still lay on the table. "My uncle told me there was a copy of it in his desk. I informed my aunt and she asked that I read it."

"I see." His thoughtful manner indicated he was sorely puzzled. "Did she have any questions concerning it?"

"Yes," I admitted. "One. It concerns the disposition of the house which, as you know, was left to me. She wishes to know if there is anything she can do about taking it from me."

"She can do nothing," he replied, regarding me carefully.

"Will you please write to her in regard to it?"

"She resents your ownership of the house then," Mr. Fillmore said.

"Yes," I replied, "and I can't blame her really. I would sign it over to her now except for one reason."

"Will you tell me what that is?"

"Gladly, because I feel you'll understand."

"I assure you," Mr. Fillmore said with a smile, "you have a sympathetic audience."

"I need one, sir," I said. "I'll be completely frank and honest. My aunt doesn't care for me. While on the way to the church, she suggested I leave this house. It was my intention to do so until I read the will to her a short time ago. Now I feel I must stay."

"Why?" came the terse question.

"Because for one thing I will never believe my uncle was intoxicated at the time of his death. For another, I believe he had a very strong motive for leaving the house to me."

Mr. Fillmore made a steeple of his fingers and regarded them thoughtfully. "I've met you only moments ago, Miss Janet, but already I have tremendous respect for your judgment. I assume you're even thinking of your father in regard to this."

"I am, sir," I said. "I don't know how I could ever find any additional information on what happened to the yacht of which he was captain. Yet my uncle believed completely in my father's innocence. He never lost an opportunity of telling me that. He told me never to let my trust waver in my father's integrity. Now I believe my uncle was trying, right up until the time of his death, to unearth some shred of evidence that would prove my father was not guilty of the horrible crime of which he was accused."

Mr. Fillmore still assumed his thoughtful position. He was silent for fully two minutes after I'd spoken. I wondered what was going through his mind and was almost afraid to hear him speak. When he finally did, his words came as quite a shock, for such a thought had never crossed my mind.

"Suppose, my dear," Mr. Fillmore said, "just suppose you are right in everything you have stated. Did the thought occur to you that your life might be in danger?"

I was amazed at his suggestion. "It sounds preposterous!"

"Perhaps," he said. "But don't you believe the charges against your uncle and your father are preposterous?"

"Yes," I said vehemently.

"In that case," he said, "I would exercise extreme caution. The bluff might be a good place to stay away from."

"I'll remember," I said with a smile. "Though I can't see why anyone would want to take my life."

"Can you think of a single reason why anyone would want to take your uncle's?"

"No," I said without a moment's hesitation.

"Yet you don't believe he was under the influence of alcohol," he stated.

"I do not," I said firmly.

"You admit he was extremely familiar with the bluff and its treacherous edge."

"I do."

"In that case, his death couldn't have been accidental."

"He was murdered?" I asked incredulously.

"I don't know," he stated. "or do you, therefore I advise you to be cautious."

"Thank you, Mr. Fillmore. I will be."

He arose. "I'm sorry I can't wait to meet Mrs. Vance.

20

But please convey my sympathies. I shall write to her, explaining in full detail the terms of the will. It is unbreakable."

"Will you also put in the letter the fact that I told you I do not intend to retain possession of this house indefinitely?"

"You mean, just between ourselves," he said as we walked slowly to the door, "you will remain here until you have solved the mystery of your uncle's death—or until you find it is unsolvable."

"That's exactly what I mean," I said. "When I leave, I shall deed the house to her."

"You're a very generous girl," he said.

"It's not that," I said thoughtfully. "My aunt deserves it. She'll get it."

At the door, I extended my hand. "Thank you, Mr. Fillmore, for coming. Also for your advice."

"Do be vigilant, my dear." Mr. Fillmore took my hand between both of his. "One thing more: if I can help you in any way, don't hesitate to call on me. Here is my card."

I slipped the proffered card into my pocket. "Thank you, sir. May I regard you as a friend?"

"You may indeed," he replied. "Just as your uncle and your father did."

"Good-bye, sir."

"Good-bye, Miss Janet." He walked to the carriage waiting at the foot of the steps, got in and waved a farewell.

I heard a door upstairs close quietly. So Nancy had been listening. In a way, I was glad. At least, she knew I wasn't conniving behind her back.

Nancy's footsteps sounded along the corridor. We met at the head of the stairs.

"Mr. Fillmore just left," I informed her.

"I saw his carriage going down the drive," she said calmly. Her hostile manner had entirely disappeared.

"I asked him about the house," I told her. "He said the will was unbreakable. He'll write you about it."

"Do you wish me to leave, my dear?" she said, her tone similar to that of a child who had been naughty and was now contrite.

"I would like you to stay," I said.

I meant it. The house was large, the area isolated and, after Mr. Fillmore's words of warning, I had no desire to live alone here.

"Thank you, my dear," she said. "Since I am, you might as well resume calling me Aunt Nancy, as you used to, before your uncle died."

I repressed a smile. "Thank you, but I'd rather not. You see, I'm quite grown up now. I would prefer us to be friends."

"I see no reason why we can't be. Though I must admit I'm hurt."

"Please don't be," I replied. "I'm going to take a walk along the cliff. The fog is lifting."

"Don't go too close to the edge," she cautioned. "And don't be gone too long. I'm going to prepare supper now. Neither of us have eaten all day. I'll fry some chicken."

"I won't be long," I promised. I went out into the slowly developing sunshine. It seemed fitting, now that the funeral was over, that the sun should come out. I walked around the house and down to the high bluff overlooking the rocky coast and the sea, which had licked the base of the bluff at high tide for generations.

The bluff walls were towering embattlements of bare, craggy stone. Like the walls of a great fortress they protected the land from the sea and would resist the erosion unto eternity, it seemed.

The foghorns had stopped their low bellowing, but the bell buoys could be heard. As the fog lifted, their tone seemed to lighten.

I knew the approximate spot from which my uncle had fallen to his death. I inspected it now, finding no trace of any part having slipped away to drop an unwary man to the rocks below. It was conceivable that, had my uncle been intoxicated, he might have fallen over. But he wasn't intoxicated and the likelihood of his having taken an incautious step was too remote to seriously consider. That left only the ominous and horrible suspicion of suicide or murder. I promptly dismissed the idea of his having killed himself, for he was not the morbid type. Only murder was left and, at the moment, it appeared as inconceivable as suicide or accident. Then I reminded myself of Mr. Fillmore's warning that I be cautious, for if my uncle had met with foul play, I could well be next.

I moved carefully, for I was still close to the bluff and the grass was slippery from the constant fog. I thought of the townsfolk, none of whom appeared at the church, and it was only with difficulty that I stifled the bitterness which threatened to flood my spirit. I knew they had avoided my uncle for months before his death, not only because they believed the ugly story of my father, but they were sick unto death, as my aunt had said, of hearing him state my father's innocence and plead for their understanding.

My thoughts shifted to the young man in the church. I knew he was a stranger in town, though I had no idea as to his identity. About that I was curious, but I was even more curious as to why he had come to the church to attend the service. Had he known my uncle? If so, why didn't he come to the house to pay his respects? I felt a sudden impatience to meet him in the hope he might have some information in regard to my uncle's death. Yet I was certain, if my uncle had known him, that he would have told me about him.

I thought of the house and once again wondered why my uncle had left it to me. It couldn't be because he feared I'd be homeless after his death. Papa had left a modest sum to me. I could take it and leave this place and use it to support myself until I had found employment of some kind. I'd thought of doing it many times while my uncle was alive. I knew now that the only thing that had kept me here was my uncle's never-ending search for some clue to prove my father's innocence. It had become an obsession with him. And as suddenly, I knew why he had left me the house. It was up to me to continue the search for the truth. I made up my mind at that moment that I would do so.

I was so intent on my thoughts that I missed my footing on a particularly slippery stretch of weeds. I cried out as I fell forward. It wasn't until then I also realized that the fog had closed in again and I had wandered near the edge so that when I fell, both hands were over the edge of the

23

cliff. My heart beat wildly as I dug my toes into the soft earth, inching myself back until my hands were on firm ground.

I finally maneuvered myself far enough from the edge so that I raised myself to my knees and, on all fours, moved still further to safer ground. Then I cautiously stood up. The front of my drees was wet and muddy. I thought of my uncle. Could the same thing have happened to him? Had he become so engrossed in his thoughts that he'd wandered close to the edge, lost his footing and gone over?

But then I remembered his statement, uttered to me many times—that only a fool would walk along the edge of the cliff during the fog, for it was certain suicide. I'd been a fool. So had Mr. Fillmore, though he hadn't been warned of its danger.

I shivered involuntarily at my narrow escape and moved with cautious footsteps back to the house.

TWO

I had hoped to gain entrance to the house without Nancy seeing me, but I was not to be so fortunate, for we met face to face in the reception hall. The rays from the lamp she was holding highlighted the moist earth clinging to my dress and my face. Her face registered amazement at my unkempt appearance.

"What happened?" she asked breathlessly.

"I walked too close to the cliff. I slipped and . . ." I paused, reluctant to tell her of what actually had happened.

"Almost went over," she finished the sentence. "And you said it couldn't have happened to Lew."

"Uncle Lew would never have gone near the edge during a fog," I replied. "You know that."

"Yes, I do," she said slowly. "Unless he was lured there."

"Who would do such a thing?" I asked, aghast at the idea.

"Only someone who knew him well," she replied, regarding me archly. "Someone whom he trusted and who betrayed that trust by throwing him over once he approached that person."

My eyes widened in astonishment. "Surely you don't suspect me of doing away with Uncle Lew!"

"I never said anyone did," she replied, her eyes never leaving my face. "You're the one who wouldn't believe his death accidental."

"I still don't," I said, still shocked at the inference of her words. "Why would I ever want to kill Uncle Lew?"

"You inherited his house, didn't you?"

"Oh please, Nancy." The inference was too absurd to upset me. "I had no idea he was going to leave the house to me. No more than you did."

"You may be assured of that. Go upstairs and change. Supper is ready."

I took the proffered lamp, wearily climbed the stairs. I was still shaken from my fall near the edge of the cliff. And now to be suspected of doing away with my uncle did nothing to ease my nerves.

In my room, I washed my hands, removed my dress, hung it up to dry, and slipped into a skirt and blouse. Though it was true I'd not eaten all day, after what Nancy had just said I had little appetite for food. Nevertheless I went downstairs. She was already seated at the kitchen table and I must say that the aroma of the food was pleasant to my nostrils. She was an excellent cook, and her fried chicken with gravy, hashed brown potatoes and fresh corn were tempting dishes. I managed to enjoy what I ate, even partaking of some apple pie and coffee. There was, however, a complete lack of conversation. I was quite aware of the ugly suspicions in her mind and I could think of no argument which would dispel it.

I was grateful to hear the clop-clop of a horse's hoofs on the stone drive. Nancy heard it at the same time and her features which had been glum, brightened.

"Who could this possibly be?" she asked.

"Not Mr. Fillmore," I replied, for lack of something to say.

"If we don't go to the door, we'll never know," she said, her tone so cheerful I almost had the idea she expected someone. Yet since the scandal regarding my father, no one ever came here.

I followed her into the reception hall, quite amazed at the briskness of her step. She must have completely forgotten about the sudden air of martyrdom she'd assumed.

She peered through a window and exclaimed, "Why, I do declare. It's Abner Pauley."

I made no comment as I glanced over her shoulder. It was Abner all right. I watched him drop the weight to the ground to tether his horse. He was a lean, almost cadaverous man, with hawk-like features which gave him the appearance of regarding everyone with suspicion. He had the reputation of being the most tight-fisted person in the village. In my opinion, he certainly did everything to earn it.

"I think it's in very bad taste his coming here today," I commented. "I can't imagine him closing the store while it's still early enough for customers."

"I know you don't like him," Nancy said. "And I know people think he's pretty close to the bark, but he's always been very generous with me. Whenever he gets something new in the store, he gives me a sample of it—without cost, I might add."

"I had no idea," I admitted. "It does come as rather a surprise."

"If you'll move out of the way, I'll open the door to welcome our guest," Nancy said.

"Forgive me." I stepped aside.

"I expect you to treat Abner with extreme courtesy."

"As he treated my uncle," I said with gentle sarcasm.

"Your uncle made a nuisance of himself, I'm sorry to say," Nancy retorted. "Now be courteous—for my sake."

She opened the door and a wide smile wreathed her face. Abner entered, holding his mouldy-looking hat in his hand.

"I have come," he said, "to offer my sympathies and condolences upon the death of your uncle." He bowed to Nancy, "And your husband, Miz Vance. Lew was a fine man."

"Come in, Mr. Pauley," Nancy said. "It's very good of you to come by. The coffee is still hot," she added, leading the way to the parlor. "May I bring you some and a piece of pie?"

"Indeed you may," he said.

"Sorry I have no cake," Nancy said. "I made some a week ago with the vanilla you gave me and it has a very unusual flavor."

"It's the newest on the market," Abner said.

Standing there watching them both behaving like adolescents I couldn't help but think how very foolish they both seemed, how very coy. Obviously such behavior was alien to both of them, yet they were trying desperately to outdo one another in graciousness. It was as if Abner had come courting.

"Janet, please keep Abner company while I get him some nourishment," Nancy said, and almost flew from the room.

Abner lost no time settling himself comfortably in a chair before the glowing fire. I stood by the mantel, for I was not at all intrigued by the company of this man and I intended to excuse myself as soon as Nancy returned. However, I was glad of the few moments alone with him, for I did have a question or two to ask and certainly he was in as good a position as anyone to answer, for every morsel of gossip in the village was passed along in his store.

"Tell me, Mr. Pauley," I said, touching upon the subject at once, "what do you think really happened to my uncle?"

He seemed startled at the frankness of the question. "I only know what they tell me. . . ."

"Did you ever see him under the influence of spirits, Mr. Pauley?"

"Can't say I did."

"The tavern is directly across the square from your store. Did you ever see my uncle go in or out of there?"

"Oh yes. Didn't make a habit of it though."

"Then why does everyone say he was drunk?"

"Thought you knew. Doc Barker says he could smell it on his breath and his clothes. Whiskey, he said it was."

"In other words, my uncle spilled whiskey all over himself before he tripped and fell over the bluff. What nonsense that is."

"Well, I find it hard to believe myself, but . . . something happened."

Nancy came in with a silver tray and service. It was the first time I'd ever seen her use it. It had been a gift from my parents, brought from some faraway place. She set this down on a table and poured the coffee. On a large plate was a huge slice of apple pie covered with a napkin. She handed Abner the plate, whipped off the napkin as if revealing the crown jewels.

He merely smiled and attacked the pie as if he hadn't eaten in days. He downed two big forkfuls of pie before he cleared his throat.

"You gonna stay here, Nancy? In this spooky old house?" he asked, and I immediately concluded the house was the matter of business which had drawn him here.

Nancy gave me a somewhat embarrassed look. "Yes, Abner, I believe I shall stay here."

"Big old house like this? No place for a young, good-looking widow woman. Advise you to sell it."

"Now who would want to buy a spooky, big old house like this?" I asked innocently.

"Might consider it myself," he said. "As an investment. Wouldn't live here you paid me. Gives me the creeps."

"It doesn't give me the creeps," I said.

"Well," Nancy said uncertainly, "it is big and it is lonely, but I've lived here for so long . . ." Her voice trailed off as if she couldn't bring herself to finish the sentence.

"Mr. Pauley," I said, "my uncle left the house to me."

Abner almost dropped the plate. "To you?"

"That's right," I said. "He left me the house and all in it. Nancy received his money and holdings. So if you're interested in purchasing the house, you will have to consult me."

"Don't imagine a young lady like yourself will want to stay in these parts," Abner reasoned.

"Why not?" I countered.

"Because . . . well . . ." He almost choked on a piece of pie and reached for his coffee to wash it down.

"Because of what the townspeople say of my father?" I prodded. "And now of my uncle?"

"Well, yes. That and the fact that you're young and oughta get out and see a bit of the world. On accounta your papa and mama travelin' all over, reckon you got sort of a gypsy foot."

"Perhaps I have a gypsy foot," I replied, trying not to show my amusement, "but for the present, I'm going to stay right here. So long as I'm near the water, I'm content. As for selling the house, I have no intention of doing so. So there's no need to discuss it further."

"No sense gettin' on your high horse," Abner complained. "Only wanted to help."

"I could use some help, I imagine," I said. "But not in selling the house. When the proper time comes, I shall no doubt deed it back to my aunt."

"What do you mean, when the proper time comes?" he asked.

"I'm not quite sure just what I mean," I replied with a sigh. "And now I must ask that you excuse me. It's been a sad day and an exhausting one. I feel quite fatigued. Good night, Mr. Pauley."

"Night, ma'am," he said, not bothering to rise. I doubted he had any knowledge of the social graces.

I excused myself to Nancy and went up to the lookout room on the third floor. I'd picked up a lamp on the second floor landing and now I set it on a table near the door. I sat down in the soft leather chair behind the desk and thought of how often I'd seen my uncle in this very chair. Wisps of fog wafted past the window, seeming like wandering spirits, drifting aimlessly. I arose and lit another lamp, dispelling some of the shadows.

It had seemed strange to learn but a few hours ago that I was now mistress of this large, bleak house. It was stranger still to have Abner Pauley come with an offer to purchase it from my aunt. What would he ever do with it? Why did he even want to buy it? Was he, in some way, connected with the mysterious events of my uncle's death? It was difficult to believe, yet it was just as difficult to hear him voice the idea of purchasing this house. He was a known tightwad. He had never, to my knowledge, parted with a dime to purchase a single piece of property in this village. Nor could I imagine him buying this house as an investment. He didn't think in those terms. He was such a miser, he had to see his money.

I had a strange feeling that things were beginning to close in on me—that there was, indeed, something very devious going on. Yet what was it and who was behind it? The young man I'd seen in the church? He'd not yet put in an appearance at the house. I wished I'd asked Abner about him, but I certainly wasn't going downstairs to question him further. If the stranger was, in any way, con-

30

nected with the mystery of my uncle's death, he would, sooner or later, put in an appearance. Until then, I must be patient.

I looked fondly upon the mementos my uncle had brought back from his voyages. These had been augmented with my father's, so that the room was littered with everything from an African drum to a wastebasket made from the leg of an Indian elephant. There were vases, metal trays, flowers under glass, everything which had attracted the attention of these seafaring men. It was a cozy room, reminding me so much of my uncle that it seemed a part of him would always be here.

I opened the desk drawers and rather aimlessly prowled through their contents. I found some old receipted bills, some ancient charts, clippings from newspapers relating to the movements of various ships. His pipes were aromatically distributed among the several drawers. The pigeonholes were empty. Uncle Lew had never been the type to pigeonhole anything. I leaned back, still mystified and somewhat disappointed that I hadn't found a clue in the desk. Had there been one, that's where he would have left it.

A sudden thought occurred to me. The pigeonhole area was separated from larger compartments by two three-inch-wide, carved miniature pillars, part of the desk design. One of these pillars could be grasped firmly, pushed hard to the left and, when released, it would spring out to expose a slot drawer, a cleverly concealed one which I used to play with as a child when Mama, Papa and I visited here.

I opened it and gasped, for I really hadn't expected to find anything. There was an envelope! Nothing else, just the thin envelope and it bore my name and the word 'personal'.

I held my breath as I slit the seal with an opener I found on the desk. I removed and unfolded the sheet of letter paper inside and began to read.

My dear Janet:

It is with the deepest reluctance that I write you this

letter, for you are much too young to be burdened with such a terrible responsibility. Circumstances, however, force me to do so because, for the last few days, I have been in fear of my life. It may be it is all in my imagination. If so, you will never find this letter. But if you do, it will be because I have met with foul play. Therefore, I feel it pertinent I impart to you what information I have. I cannot tell Nancy, for as you know her sympathies were not with me in my opinion that your father was terribly wronged. I dare not write my attorney Mr. Fillmore, lest he think me a fool. Which leaves no one but you, my dear niece, whose gracious companionship filled my lonely hours. But I must get on with this and I pray that, should something happen to me, you will come up here with thoughts of me and chance will lead you to find this letter.

You know I have never believed your father lost his ship because of drunkenness and carelessness. Such an idea is too preposterous to even consider. I don't know what happened, to a degree where I might try to give some facts, but I have strong suspicions.

I have carefully charted the course of the yacht he captained. I have considered its speed, the time of the wireless message, the weather and wind. In my opinion, the yacht must have been very close to the bluff upon which my house is built. Remember, its designation was but twenty-six miles north. If the ship was in trouble, your father would have made for our village port if he was close by, as I believe he was.

Now the night it happened, the sea was fairly calm, but it was a black night. Also a warm night and I spent it on the widow's walk above you. I thought I heard voices that night. They seemed to come in on the wind, but I was never sure. The next morning, I investigated, but I saw nothing to indicate a ship had been out there. I tried to plot the location of the faint voices and it seemed they came from a position due east of the lone poplar that stands near the edge of the bluff. Trying to plot the location of voices at sea is difficult enough, but I wasn't even sure there had been any.

Yet my curiosity was aroused and it stayed alive for many months, though without the slightest result. One week ago I was enjoying one of my daily walks at the foot of the bluff when I saw a bit of wood sticking out of the sand. It didn't look like driftwood so I gave it a pull and it stuck there. I was curious enough to get a shovel and, in a little while, I uncovered the remnants of a lifeboat. It had been burned, but the prow had resisted the flames. However the sea must have washed it deep and the sand covered it. The name on the lifeboat was the name of the yacht your father captained. The night of the sinking, I'd been right. There had been something out there and someone had come ashore.

I made inquiries to find out if any strangers were seen around the village, but I learned nothing. However, I had reburied the lifeboat. When I returned, I found evidence that someone had been looking for it. The following day, while I walked below the bluff, a huge rock seemed to come loose and it almost crashed on me as it fell. I happened to know that particular rock and I discovered it had been pried loose. I found evidence of that. So I fear for my life, thought I don't know what the answer to all of this can be.

Should anything happen to me, you are the only person who might use this information. If you do, take care. I think there is evil here. I don't know why or who, I don't even know what happened, but it seems someone is afraid I may find out. So I am writing a new will, leaving the house and all in it to you, so that if you choose you may remain close to the bluff and the beach, for that is where the answer must lie.

I pray that I am not making a grave mistake in passing on this information and thus exposing you to danger. Yet I feel that if there is the slightest chance of clearing your father's name, you will want to do so.

I have faith in your courage and I know you will endeavor to uncover whatever dastardly evil destroyed your father and, perhaps me. I suggest you burn this letter. Trust no one, and above all, be on guard.

I know you have no friends in this town. I know the agony and humiliation you have been subjected to. Should you suddenly acquire friends, whether they are new to this village or have lived here a long time, exercise extreme vigilance.

With deep affection,

Uncle Lew

I fumbled in one of the drawers to find matches. I struck one, touched the flame to the edge of the letter and let it burn. I destroyed the envelope in the same way.

So there had been something to my suspicions. Uncle Lew had never been given to flights of fancy. I found some solid consolation in the letter, for it bore out my own ideas, and it gave me an urgent desire and determination to find the proof that my father and my uncle were men worthy of their titles and their seamanship.

I resolved to follow Uncle Lew's advice and say nothing about this to anyone—particularly not to Nancy. Quite likely she'd scoff at the whole idea. Or if she didn't, she'd probably run to Abner with the story.

I felt restless and also the need for some exercise. I went outside the room and climbed the ladder to the widow's walk. The fog was rapidly being dissipated now with a wind that, though gentle, was persistent. Occasionally a wisp of its wetness brushed against my cheek. I stood on the deck and leaned against the rail, listening to the pounding of the surf against the rocks. I filled my lungs with the salty air. Strangely, I felt no fear. There was even now a hint of moonlight and I found myself looking out to sea, in a line directly behind that poplar which stood like some darker shadow against the shades of night over the ocean.

34

I had no idea how long I stood there, but it must have been for some time. Here I felt at peace with myself, filled with the resolve to clear the name of my father and my uncle, if it were possible to do so.

Something glistened far out on the water. I turned my head away, then looked back. It was still there, blinking slightly like a light that rolled with the mild waves. It had a reddish glow, an eerie sort of thing that had no business at that distance where there was nothing but water.

Very faintly, I heard what seemed to be a cry—a human cry, yet hollow and melancholy. Distant and tremulous, but still it sounded real. I turned my head to hear better.

"Jannnnn . . . etttt. . . . !" The voice calling my name drifted eerily in on the wind. "Jannn . . . etttt . . . !"

I gave a sharp cry of fear. The reddish pinpoints of light were still there. The voice reached me again and again, a doleful cry that sounded as if it came from space itself. In my imagination, inspired by fear or hope—I didn't know which—I thought it sounded like the voice of my father as I remembered it. I knew it couldn't be; my common sense told me so. Yet when the voice repeated my name over and over, I knew I wanted it to be he. I wanted to believe him alive. Could such a thing be possible?

Once I even raised my hands, cupped them to my lips and was ready to cry out in answer until I realized the futility and the foolishness of such a gesture.

Was I losing my sanity? I wondered. Was someone trying to frighten me? If so, who and why? Those questions would trouble me over and over in the days to come. I went down the ladder and entered my uncle's room. There I blew out one lamp and picked up the other to lighten my way. I needed rest and sleep, for there was much for me to do . . . much for me to learn.

One question had already been answered for me: my uncle had met with foul play. His letter assured me of that. It was up to me to see that the murderer was brought to justice.

THREE

I lay in bed, still shaken by that voice coming over the water calling my name. It must have been all of two hours since I'd blown out the lamp and I sorely needed sleep, but my mind was fiercely active as it attempted to find the answers to questions which troubled me. I thought of my uncle's dismal funeral, attended only by two strangers, one of whom I'd still to meet. Then Abner Pauley's surprising visit to this house with an offer to purchase it, plus his surprise when he'd learned my uncle had willed it to me. There was the finding of my uncle's letter and, last of all, the small red lights at sea, accompanied by the spectral voice wafted to shore, calling my name.

Tomorrow morning I would rise early and inspect the beach in the area where my uncle had located the lifeboat with the name *Cecelia* on it. The burned lifeboat would be tangible proof that the *Cecelia* had sunk close by and that one or more persons had escaped the tragedy. Yet if such was the case, why didn't they come forward?

I thought of the young stranger in church and wondered about his presence there. Would I meet him again? I wanted to, for he might be able to enlighten me in some way. If the young man had any part in this mystery, he would soon make his presence known.

My first duty was to seek out and uncover the burned hull of the lifeboat. At least, I had something to go on. The thought comforted me and I pulled the covers closer about my neck, snuggled my head deeper into the feather pillow and gradually drifted off to sleep.

How long I slept, I don't know, but when I awakened it was still dark, and I felt prickles of fear course through me. A sound of some kind had awakened me and I lay there, in the coolness of the night, breaking out in a mild sweat of apprehension. Then it came again . . . someone was moving about downstairs. The steps were slow, methodical, reminding me somewhat of the way Papa used to pace the floor when he had been unable to sleep. Up and down, the captain on his bridge, pacing its limited area.

I threw back the covers, fumbled on the table for matches and got a lamp lit. I put on slippers and a wrapper, lit a lamp and, calling upon all my courage, I stepped into the upstairs corridor and stood there, the lamp held high.

A loud creak was followed by the gentle opening or closing of a downstairs door. It could have been my imagination, but I didn't believe so. I moved to the head of the stairs and paused. I felt a sudden draft of cool night air sweeping up the stairwell. It stirred my wrapper, brushing it against my ankles. A moment later, I thought I heard the front door click shut. I moved down the stairs now and tried the door. It was locked. Yet someone could have used a key. I opened the door to darkness, broken only by the now-wavering flame of my lamp. I was turning away when I saw the dark spots on the floor of the veranda. I bent down, holding the lamp closer. There was wet sand on the porch, spaced as if it had come from the shoes of someone who'd walked the beach. Or had come out of the sea!

I stifled a scream and backed into the house, closing the door quickly and bolting it. I turned around and saw a figure standing on the stairs. I cried out, then realized it was Nancy. I set the lamp down on a table and grasped the newel post to support myself, for I was trembling.

"What is it?" Nancy asked, moving slowly down the stairs.

"I don't know," I gasped. "Truly, I don't know."

"Why are you trying to frighten me?" she asked, half in anger, half in fear.

"I'm not, Nancy, truly I'm not!" My voice pleaded with her to believe me. "I heard a sound—I was awakened by footsteps downstairs. At least, I thought they were footsteps. I didn't even think of who it might be. I lit a lamp and came out into the corridor. It was in darkness. Just as I reached the head of the stairs, I'm positive I heard the door close."

Nancy's hand went to her throat. "Did you see anyone?"

"No," I replied. I could feel some of the fear and tension drain from me as I talked. "But I went out on the veranda. I . . . I saw . . ." I paused, not wanting to finish, fearful she would ridicule me.

"Go on, Janet," she urged. "Tell me what you saw."

"There were wet footsteps out there. Sandy ones, as if someone had been walking along the beach."

"Or had come out of the sea," Nancy said solemnly, her eyes staring into space as if she was even now visualizing it.

"Please, Nancy!" I said. My nerves had quieted now that I had someone to talk to, and my thinking became more lucid. "I heard the door close. It was no spirit. It was a human being who entered this house."

"You saw no one," she contradicted. "You said that."

"There was no light downstairs," I argued. "My eyes could scarcely pierce the darkness."

"Why did you scream when you saw me?"

"I didn't recognize you at first," I told her.

"You wanted to frighten me, didn't you?" she said. Her hands gripped my shoulders and she shook me. "Didn't you?"

"No, Nancy, I didn't," I argued frantically. "I swear I didn't!"

"You're trying to drive me from this house!" Her voice rose in anger.

"I'm not!" I protested. "I'd be frightened to live here alone. I'm grateful you're staying."

She released her hold on me, but her eyes still revealed their disbelief.

I pointed a finger at the door which I'd bolted. "If you don't believe what I've told you, go out and look at the damp, sandy footsteps."

"I'll do no such thing," she said. Then, her tone softening, she added, "Abner's right. Two women should not be

38

in this house without protection."

"I'd like to know why Abner Pauley feels we need protection. He saw nothing amiss about Uncle Lew's death."

"Why should he? It was an accident. Everyone believes it except you. Do you still believe it was not an accident?"

I thought of the letter, yet my lips were, of necessity, sealed. "I don't know what to believe," I said wearily. "In any case, I've bolted the door."

"That wouldn't keep the spirit of your father or your uncle out," she said remindfully.

"No," I agreed. "That's why I know it wasn't a spirit. Spirits don't open or close doors. I'm positive I heard the door close. I felt the draft of cold air on my ankles."

"I'd far rather it be a specter than a human," Nancy said, regarding the closed door.

"I suppose I would myself," I said thoughtfully. "At least, a ghost has never been known to do anyone harm. If one believes in them, which I don't."

"I do." Nancy regarded me coldly. "This afternoon when you fell . . . you near the edge of the cliff?"

"Yes," I admitted. "My hands hung over the side. Had I slid a matter of inches, I'd have gone over."

"Was anyone around?"

"What are you trying to say?" I asked, completely puzzled by her questions.

"Did anyone see you fall?"

"No."

"Perhaps you just said you fell," she replied archly. "It would be easy enough for you to pick up wet earth and smear it on your dress."

"For what purpose?" I asked, my manner now as cold as hers.

"To frighten me."

"Why should I want to frighten you?" I demanded.

"To drive me from this house," she replied. "Who knows, even I might end up at the bottom of the cliff."

I shook my head in utter dismay. "Surely you don't believe I would want to do away with you. I can't imagine what put such a thought into your head."

"I believe I shall ask Abner to come here and put a bolt on my bedroom door," she said.

"So it was Abner who suggested you beware of me," I said, my manner scornful. "I don't like to bring this point up, Nancy, but the ugly suspicion Abner has implanted in your mind forces me. This is now my home. I think it was in extremely bad taste for him to come here immediately following Uncle Lew's funeral for the sole purpose of making an offer to purchase the house."

"I feel he is a friend in need," Nancy retorted. "And he is welcomed to come here to pay his respects—whenever he wishes and as often as he wishes."

"Not if he continues to poison your mind against me," I retorted. "Remember that, Nancy!"

"You're trying to drive me out of this house!"

"I'm not," I said wearily, "and I'll not argue further with you. I'm tired and I need sleep."

"I'll put a chair against my door for protection," she said meaningfully.

"I think you're wise." I picked up the lamp and moved to the stairway.

She stepped to one side and let me precede her. I knew the move was deliberate, as if she didn't trust me behind her. I entered my room, not even holding the lamp to light her way. If she feared me, it would be wiser to let her see I had no desire to watch her every move. Yet, somehow, I couldn't believe she really thought I would murder her. By the same token, I couldn't imagine Abner planting such an ugly suspicion in her mind, nor his reason for doing so.

Once again in my bed, I let myself go limp. I had no desire to dwell on further unpleasantness. I turned the lamp low so that, while the room was shadowy, I was not in darkness. Thus reassured, I once again drifted off into sleep.

It was barely dawn when I awakened. I dressed quickly, slipped a shawl over my shoulders, and made my silent way out of the house, heading directly for the bluff. I moved cautiously over the ground, for it was slippery from the dew. I didn't want another fall.

I approached the poplar my uncle had referred to in his letter so that I could look out to sea from that point. I stood there awhile, trying to visualize what might have happened out there, but it was hopeless, for the sea never

40

revealed its secrets. I had much to do today and could waste no further time with my imaginings, so I moved along to the footpath leading down to the beach. There were steps carved out of the rocky cliff which spiraled down to the beach, but I knew they'd be slippery and the descent would be too treacherous in the half-light of dawn.

I reached the beach and moved slowly, my eyes searching for some sign of where the boat my uncle had spoken of in his letter might be buried. I was attracted to a small strip of canvas which had apparently caught on a bush. A close check revealed that it had been pushed down over the spiked top of the broken branch. A tinge of nervous excitement coursed through me at the discovery. I felt certain Uncle Lew had placed it there as a clue to the spot where the boat lay buried.

It was a rocky area and I immediately began digging and scooping out handfuls of sand. I kept at it until one of my hands scraped against something rough. Cautiously now, I continued moving the earth until I had exposed the bow of a lifeboat. Scarcely able to breathe from the excitement of my discovery, I kept on with my work until I was able to see some letters painted on the side. They had been almost obliterated by time and the elements, but I could still read the name *Cecilia*. That was the name of the yacht my father had commanded on his last voyage!

I hastily covered the burned and broken hull until it was again hidden. I looked around, suddenly fearful I might have been observed. I well knew the pounding of the surf would have prevented my hearing anyone approach. But there was no one visible and I breathed a sigh of relief as I headed for the spiral staircase cut out of the rocks. The sun had broken over the horizon and I had no fear of ascending the craggy cliff. It was the shorter way up and I wished to return to the house in the hope I could regain my room without Nancy having any awareness that I'd been abroad.

This time I was more fortunate. The house was soundless. Nancy was nowhere in sight. I washed my hands, cleaned my nails of the sand embedded beneath them, and donned my nightdress. I was going to rest awhile, for I'd had little sleep and what I was about to do would require all the stamina I possessed.

It was midmorning when I awakened, thoroughly rested, eager to carry out the task I'd set for myself. I dressed, brushed my hair, put it up as carefully as if I were going into town and went downstairs to breakfast. I knew Nancy had already eaten so I prepared bacon and eggs. The coffee, still hot, sat on the back of the stove. I made two slices of toast in the oven and ate heartily of the food I'd prepared.

Nancy entered the kitchen just as I was drying the last dish. I greeted her cheerily, as if I had no memory of her harsh words of a few hours ago. She returned the greeting, but there was neither warmth nor friendliness in her tone. She resented my presence in this house and made no effort to hide it.

I left the house, grateful for the bright sunlight. It seemed a fitting omen and I noticed the grass underfoot was free of the heavy dew of early morn. That meant I could use the steps which had been carved out of the rocky cliff. It was more to my liking for I could save time. It was also handy to the boathouse which held Uncle Lew's dory. I had two bathing suits there and I couldn't wait to change into one and get the dory into the water. It was an excellent boat which could be rigged for sail if need be.

I quickly changed into my bathing suit and covered my hair with a bathing cap. I dragged the dory out of the boathouse, down to the edge of the water and, with a quick push, drove it afloat. I jumped in, picked up the oars and slipped them into place. Then I set my back to it and pulled steadily, all the while keeping my eyes on the poplar on the bluff, staying directly in line with it. When I judged about where I'd seen the lights last night, I shipped the oars and peered overside.

It was past midmorning, the sun high enough to penetrate some of the blackness below the water. I saw nothing at first, letting the dory drift as it would. The tide was incoming and I was being carried ashore. Therefore, I manned the oars again, rowed further out, then let the boat drift once more. I kept my head over the rail while lying

42

flat in the boat so I could peer as deeply beneath the surface as possible.

Then I saw something. It was only a darker shadow, well below the range of the sunlight, but it had a shape and therefore must have a considerable substance and not be merely a large piece of driftwood. I doubted the water was too deep at this spot. A risky enough dive, but I was expert at it. I was a competent swimmer, a good diver, and I had a fine lung capacity for endurance.

Whatever lay below must be investigated immediately. I slipped over the side of the boat, swam around a bit, now and then going under. It was fairly easy to see the large, dark shadow below.

I wondered if I was being observed by anyone. Regardless, I was going to dive. I took a long breath and went under. All I wanted to do at this time was to make some physical contact with that dark shape. It might be an illusion, a piece of jetsam, even the old wreck off some other ship. I prayed it would be the *Cecelia*.

I couldn't quite make it, so I surfaced and dived again with a fresh supply of oxygen in my lungs. This time I went much deeper and, for just one bare instant, my fingertips touched something rough and solid. I came to the surface, located the dory and began to swim toward it. I had nearly reached it when I became aware of a great splashing nearby. The next moment I was seized about the waist by a pair of hands. Immediately, I struggled, sputtered and freed myself from their grip. When I turned, I was looking directly at the stranger who'd been in the church yesterday. His face was no more than six inches from mine and, at the moment, it was clearly etched with concern. Whether or not for me, I had no idea.

"What were you trying to do, drown me?" I asked, taking no pains to hide my anger.

"Sorry, miss," came the reply. "I thought you were in trouble."

"I was swimming to my dory," I said impatiently. "Didn't you see it?"

"Oh, I saw the boat all right," he said. "I just didn't see anyone in it. Then when you surfaced, I felt I was about to be a hero."

43

"Sorry to disappoint you," I said, already captivated by his contagious smile. "But I happen to have been raised in the water."

"My apologies," he said. "Would you mind giving me a ride back? I'll ply the oars."

"Come along," I said.

The stranger held the boat while I got in it, then he agilely climbed aboard.

"The next time," he said, "it might be a good idea to drop anchor. You might have been stranded out here."

"I'll remember," I said, removing my bathing cap so I could hear better. I believed I could have managed to get ashore, even if the dory had drifted away, but I wisely remained silent. I'd thought him good looking when I saw him in the church. Now I decided he was handsome. I suppose it was his eyes, so clear and blue and sincere.

"Where did you come from?" I asked.

"Not far from here. Forgive me. My name is Jeff Cameron. I'm a lobsterman."

"How do you do, Mr. Cameron," I said. "I am Miss Janet Vance."

"I know. I saw you in church. I'm truly sorry about the death of your uncle."

I sobered. "Did you know him?"

"Only briefly. But I liked him. That's why I attended his funeral."

"Thank you." I was touched by his quiet sincerity. "I saw you at the church and wondered who you were."

"I wanted to go to your home and express my sympathy, but I didn't know whether or not it would displease your aunt."

"It wouldn't have," I assured him. "It's comforting to know there is one person in the village who has kind thoughts about Uncle Lew."

"Your uncle should have been given the benefit of the doubt—as well as your father," he said.

"So you know about my father also."

"Only what your uncle told me."

"I guess he told everyone who would give him an audience."

"Do you blame him?"

44

"No. He never believed my father guilty."

"Nor did I, even before I met his daughter."

I could feel the color rush to my cheeks and I felt rather a fool. It was a gracious compliment, though certainly not one which should make me blush. I decided to turn the conversation away from myself.

"You're really a stranger to the village, aren't you, Mr. Cameron?"

"I arrived here a week ago. I have a shack below Blue Cove. My traps are strung out all the way north to the point and down below this beach."

"You don't speak at all like a native," I said, wondering exactly where he did come from and why he had chosen this particular spot.

"Well, I've had quite a bit of schooling. Just happens I like the sea and I find lobstering fun and also profitable. Anything else you'd like to ask me, Miss Vance?"

He'd succeeded in embarrassing me even though his smile had taken some of the sting out of his words.

"I apologize," I said. "I was prying, but in view of what happened to my uncle, I believe I have every right to be suspicious of a stranger."

"You mean," he reasoned, "you suspect your uncle met with foul play."

"I do," I said, without a moment's hesitation.

"Can you think of a motive?"

I could, but I couldn't voice it, so I merely said, "Sometimes murder doesn't need a motive."

"There usually is one though," he argued quietly.

"True." I noted that he handled the oars expertly. He had a splendid physique and was in excellent trim.

"Miss Vance, I'll tell you something that may surprise you."

"I doubt anything would surprise me," I said thoughtfully.

"Let's see if this will. I don't believe your uncle was drunk the night he supposedly fell off the cliff. I don't believe your uncle ever drank to the point of drunkenness."

"You have surprised me, Mr. Cameron," I said. "Just what do you believe happened to my uncle?"

45

"I believe he was knocked unconscious. That whiskey was spilled down his throat and all over his clothes after which he was thrown off the cliff onto the rocks below."

"Why do you believe this?" I asked earnestly.

"I was in his company three times," Mr. Cameron said. "At the village tavern. Each time I came in, he was sitting at a table alone. I asked him if I might join him. He wasn't drinking when I joined him and each time he and I had but one rum. He wasn't a drinking man any more than I am."

"I'm pleased to hear you say that, though I always knew it."

"I'm grateful for the opportunity to say it," Mr. Cameron replied. "I'd like to tell your aunt the same thing."

I repressed a smile that would only have been bitter. "Please don't. You might not convince her. She's deeply hurt at the treatment she received from the villagers, though she feels my uncle brought it all on himself. This is a difficult time for her and I think it would be wise just now to say nothing about it."

"I'm not sure I understand, but I'll follow your advice. You see, I want very much to see more of you."

I regarded him curiously and I remembered Uncle Lew's warning against confiding in anyone. Was this young man trying to win my confidence by taking sides with me? He knew I was ostracized by the town, just as he knew my uncle had been, and all because of my father. What was Jeff Cameron's interest in me? He undoubtedly had been watching me on the water. Had he seen me this morning when I uncovered the lifeboat? A cold wave of apprehension overcame me and I shivered involuntarily.

He noticed and said, "I'd better get you back," and started to row faster.

"I do feel a mite cold," I said. "I have a change of clothes in the boathouse."

"Good," he said. "I'd like to present you with some lobsters for your supper tonight."

"How nice," I replied. "My aunt will appreciate that."

"Four to be exact," he said, in mock seriousness. "If you would consider inviting me."

46

"You're invited," I said, laughing. "My aunt's an excellent cook. She does well with lobsters and I believe she'll be pleased to make your acquaintance."

I wasn't the least bit surprised, when he guided the dory directly under the boathouse, to notice his lobster boat anchored outside. He assisted me from the boat and I went up the stairs into the room built above the water. I closed the door, slipped out of my wet suit, toweled myself and dressed quickly. There was a cracked mirror on the wall and I tucked a few wisps of my jet black hair into place. I noticed my cheeks had high color, but I attributed it to my swim. My gray eyes sparkled and I attributed that to the discovery I'd made when I dove beneath the surface of the water. If only the sunken wreck was the yacht *Cecelia*.

I took my shawl from a wall peg and slipped it over my shoulders. Though the day was balmy, there was a coolness to the breeze which blew in from the Atlantic. I went down the stairs and walked along the plank to the small pier. Mr. Cameron was standing in the boat, awaiting me.

"I have some cold lobster and excellent sauce, if you'll do me the honor," he said. "I'm not far from here."

"I'd be delighted," I said. "I'm really famished."

"Then let's go." He assisted me into the boat and I took my seat forward. He rowed and it took only minutes to reach the inlet where his shack was located.

It proved to be something more than that, being a one-room structure, but weathertight and pleasantly, though sparsely, furnished. It was spotless and it had a small veranda which was partially closed in to give protection from the wind. There was a table and a chair on either side of it, and it appeared that he ate most of his meals there. In any case, that was where we dined. He insisted on preparing the dishes himself and when he brought them out, they presented a colorful, appetizing picture of crisp lettuce topped with large pieces of cold lobster. The large dish of sauce was just tangy enough and had a delicious flavor. There were also rolls, butter and hot coffee. I didn't leave a morsel of food on my plate.

While we ate, we limited our conversation to the village, and how the seacoast of Maine was becoming more and more of a resort area, though the season didn't start until July. It was still only mid-June and I knew that whatever I hoped to accomplish must be done before the vacationers came. Not that there were very many, for there were few accommodations, but I needed as much quiet and privacy as possible to uncover the mystery of the sunken yacht and the death of my uncle.

As if my thoughts had been transmitted to my host, he said, "Let me help you, Miss Vance." He spoke with such seriousness, I was startled, for our conversation, up to that moment, had been both light and pointless.

"I don't know what you mean," I replied in all innocence.

"Oh yes, you do. You believe there's a wreck out there. You were trying to find it when I surprised you."

"You're talking nonsense," I said. I touched my napkin to my lips and started to arise.

He reached over and his hand covered mine which rested on the table. "Just a minute, Janet," he said. Then, noticing my hostile look, he added, "So I'm getting personal. I want to see a lot of you and I detest formality. Neither do I like practicing deceit. Everyone knows about the *Cecelia*. Your uncle discussed it with me. Why won't you?"

I again recalled the warning in my uncle's letter, stating that I should tell no one of what he revealed in his letter to me. Also, he had cautioned me not to trust anyone—neither villagers nor strangers. This young man certainly fell into the latter category. Besides which, he had certainly gone out of his way to become acquainted.

"For one who dislikes deceit," I said coldly, "I would say you are quite adept at practicing it."

"You mean my attempt to rescue you from drowning."

"I was not drowning," I contradicted. "I was in no trouble."

"Very well," he admitted, releasing my hand. "I decided it was as good a way as any to meet you."

"Why did you feel the need to meet me?" I countered.

He frowned, then shrugged. "I like you. When I saw you in the church that day, I felt you could use a friend."

48

"I could," I said. "But not one who indulges in subterfuge as well as deceit."

"In that case, we're both guilty, aren't we?"

"Perhaps," I admitted, "though for different reasons. You see, I don't usually make friends so easily."

His expression was quizzical as he replied, "Very well, Miss Vance. I'll accept your reason. I know you're a lady and most discreet. But let me say this. Should you, at any time, feel the need for help, please call on me."

"Thank you, Mr. Cameron," I replied politely. "I will."

"And now about those lobsters. I'll get them, but I won't force my company on you for supper."

"Oh, please come," I said, suddenly fearful I might not see him again. It could well be I might learn something from him. "My uncle's widow will want to meet you."

"Don't you ever refer to her as your aunt?" I was beginning to find his directness an embarrassment.

"I would, except that she doesn't particularly care for me."

"Because your uncle left you the house?"

"You know about that?" I asked, completely surprised.

"Oh come now, Miss Vance, you don't think Abner Pauley lost any time passing that information around."

"I suppose not," I admitted. "I just hadn't thought about it."

"Suppose you go down to the boat and wait there. I'm going to change."

I moved leisurely down to the boat, my mind filled with thoughts of Jeff Cameron. I liked him. I felt he was trustworthy, though I dared not confide in him—he might be a very clever young man, here for the very purpose of gaining my confidence, putting me off guard. That must never happen. I was glad though for the company of someone my own age. Perhaps, as we grew better acquainted, I would know if he was worthy of my trust. In the meantime I at least had companionship, and that I sorely needed.

He joined me and his garb was certainly not that of a native, for he was wearing spotless white flannel trousers

49

and a blue sweater striped with white at the neck.

He rowed well and quickly so that we soon found ourselves at the beach below the spiral stairway. He pulled
the boat all the way out of the water, slipped the pail over
his arm, took my elbow with his other hand and led me to
the steps. We scaled the steep incline cut into the face
of the bluff and at the top he stood looking out to sea while
the late afternoon sunlight sparkled below us.

I wondered what he was thinking. At the same time, I
was fearful he might attempt to question me again. I knew
he was direct and clever and I couldn't help but feel that
his reason for forcing a meeting was more than just a
desire to become acquainted with me. If I was right, then I
would certainly do nothing to discourage his attention.
Only in that way would I learn whether he was friend or
enemy.

At the house, Nancy was plainly surprised that I'd
brought a guest. But her manner was courteous and when
she saw the lobsters Mr. Cameron had brought, she even
became pleasant. She exclaimed over them, rushed into
the kitchen to get a large vat of water boiling. She insisted
on attending to everything, even to making biscuits, and
suggested I show Mr. Cameron about the house.

I did just that, finally taking him up to the room atop
the house. He was plainly astounded at the view and very
complimentary in regard to the furnishings in the room.

"You can see in every direction from here," he said.
"As far out to sea as the eye can reach. With a glass you
could watch everyone in the village. Quite a paradise for a
gossip who wished to spy on others."

We sat down to the lobster supper which was delicious.
Even Nancy seemed gregarious and pleasant. Afterwards
Jeff and I walked in the dusk, along the garden paths and
all the way to the bluff and back.

We paused at the foot of the steps and I extended my
hand in a gesture of friendship.

"It's been a pleasant day and I hate it to end," Jeff said,
"but I'm up before dawn and I've many traps to tend
tomorrow. May I come back?"

"Whenever you wish," I said warmly. "I've enjoyed

50

your company. And . . . I'd like you to call me Janet."

"Ah!" His face broke into a wide smile. He squeezed my hand slightly, then released it. "You know, I sensed I was your guest on a trial basis, but I believe I've passed the test and that from now on we'll be friends."

"Thank you, Mr. Cameron," I said.

"Then you'll have to be less formal and call me Jeff."

"Jeff," I spoke the name slowly, liking the sound of it.

"Janet and Jeff sort of go together, don't you think?" he asked, regarding me seriously.

"The way you say them makes it seem so," I replied, lowering my eyes for fear that, even in the darkness, they might reveal how great an impression this young man had already made on me. "I must go in now. Good night."

"Good night, dear Janet," he said. "I'll dream of you."

I turned and moved up the stairs quickly, not stopping until I was inside the house and had closed the door behind me, for as he spoke he had moved closer and I was fearful his arms were about to enclose me. I leaned against the door until the wild beating of my heart returned to a normalcy that would permit me to enter the parlor where I knew Nancy would be awaiting my return.

"Janet?" she called. I was amazed at the friendliness in her tone.

"Coming, Nancy," I replied, hoping the inner excitement I felt would not be revealed in my face.

She was sitting beside the glowing fireplace, and spoke as I entered the room. "Strange we never met Mr. Cameron before."

"He's new here," I told her. "He met Uncle Lew in the village a few times."

"Strange Lew never mentioned him," she said, frowning.

"I believe their acquaintanceship was brief," I said. "Perhaps a week or so before Uncle Lew's death."

"And Mr. Cameron is lobstering just north of here?"

"Yes," I told her, pleased at her interest.

She regarded me curiously. "I know you're a very discreet person, Janet, one who is well-versed in the social graces. So you'll understand why I'm wondering how you met."

I smiled. "I was swimming today. He saw me and thought I might be in difficulty. He swam out to where I was."

She nodded, apparently satisfied. "I like him. I'm glad you have a friend your age. Oh, I realize he's a few years your senior, but he's still very young. I don't like you to be lonely. It's not good for anyone."

"I agree," I said, now more than a little puzzled myself. She'd never before expressed either solicitude or interest in my life.

"Abner came by today," she said. "I was pleased to see him. He seemed most concerned about me. He asked if he could come again and I gave my permission."

My face must have revealed my surprise, and perhaps even my disapproval. Not because she was seeing Abner Pauley, but that she'd be interested in having him come so soon after my uncle's strange death.

"Oh, you're probably shocked," she said with a sigh. "But I hope you won't forbid his coming here."

"Of course I won't," I assured her.

"You know, Janet, your uncle was not one to believe a person should mourn a lost one too long," she said.

I didn't think a matter of twenty-four hours was too long, but if she was romantically interested in Abner Pauley, or merely desired his friendship, it was her affair. Nothing could bring my uncle back. Also, I thought, perhaps she welcomed the idea of a man coming by from time to time. It was lonely here now.

"I'm sure you'll also agree," she continued, "that supper tonight was a much more cheerful meal with Mr. Cameron than if there'd been just the two of us."

"I do agree," I said.

She seemed quite pleased by my reply. I wondered if Abner had made any further mention of purchasing the house, but I knew better than to ask. The atmosphere was, for once, pleasant and compatible. I'd do nothing to change it.

We retired at nine and I told Nancy to run along, that I'd check to see the door and windows were locked. She regarded me curiously and I wished I'd not said anything to bring to mind the event of the night before when I'd been awakened by sounds downstairs and, investigating, discovered the wet, sandy footsteps on the veranda floor.

"I told Abner about what you heard," she said, as if reading my mind.

"I also saw the footsteps," I told her.

"I mentioned them," she said. "I must say this, Janet. I looked for them this morning when I arose, but there wasn't even a grain of sand on the porch."

"The sun could have dried the sand," I reasoned, annoyed with myself that I'd never thought to check in daylight.

"It could have," she said. "But the sand would have still been there, for no breeze had come up to blow it away."

"Don't you believe what I told you, Nancy?" I asked.

She gave an impatient shake of her head. "I can't answer that, Janet. Or rather, I won't."

She arose and started to leave the room, but I stepped before her, blocking her path. "Do you really believe I would try to frighten you—or even worse, do you harm?"

"Please step out of my way," she said, her tone assuming the coldness to which I was accustomed. "I hope you wouldn't. After all, I was your uncle's wife for many years. But then, he died mysteriously, didn't he?"

"Yes," I said bluntly. "I'm glad you finally admit it. Up until now, everyone, including yourself, attributed his death to an accident caused by his gross drunkenness."

There was such undiluted hatred in her eyes that I thought, for a moment, she was going to strike me. Her hand did rise, but paused in midair. Then she brushed past me and I heard her footsteps stop only long enough for her to pick up a lamp in the hall to light her way up the darkened stairway.

My sigh was one of resignation as I went to check the doors and windows. Not that it would do any good if someone really wished to gain access to the house, but at least he might make himself heard and it would serve as a warning. Yet what good would that do, I wondered. How could I protect either Nancy or myself?

I went up the stairs slowly, the lamp I was holding throwing eerie shadows along the walls but I was too preoccupied by my own problems to notice. The momentary comfort I'd felt by my aunt's apparent friendliness had gone. Our relationship was as it had been.

I heard the sound of something heavy being moved and I knew she had pushed a heavy object against her bedroom door. She actually did fear me.

Once in my room I thought of Jeff, and wondered if I'd done the wise thing in not confiding in him. If I followed the dictates of my heart, I'd have told him everything I knew, including the contents of the letter, for I knew I was growing fond of him. But I couldn't let my emotions rule me.

Yet it was good to know I had a friend. I'd not believe him capable of deceit until I had proof. With that thought in mind, I extinguished the lamp and, in minutes, blessed sleep overtook me.

FOUR

Unless there was a fierce wind, or the night was stormy, I always slept with one window open a few inches, for I loved the tangy smell of the sea. Tonight was no exception, yet a wind had apparently risen, for I was awakened by a current of air blowing through the room. At least, that's what I thought when my eyes first opened.

I settled back, to once again court sleep, though I seemed to be alert, as if listening for something. Yet all I heard was the distant pounding of the surf against the rocks. I sat up, reached for my wrapper and slipped it on. I pushed my feet into my soft-soled crocheted slippers and went over to sit beside the open window, making no attempt to close it, for the breeze was not a cold one.

I looked out at the sea and as my eyes accustomed themselves to the darkness, I was able to make out the whitecaps, for it was mildly rough tonight. The wind was sighing in the tamaracks and hissing through the ash trees which formed a windbreak to the north of the house. Sometimes, when the wind was very high, it seemed to actually sob along the row of firs.

Its lament was but a momentary abstraction, for my mind was concerned entirely with Jeff Cameron. I couldn't seem to shut him out of my mind and I was troubled, for the clever way he had managed an introduction was a nagging thought in the back of my mind. He was intelligent, charming and well-schooled. I somehow had the feeling he wasn't what he seemed to be—rather, what he'd said he was, a lobsterman. Both his speech and his dress seemed to give the lie to everything he'd told me about himself. Yet why would he want to lie? I was about

55

to arise and return to my bed when prickles of fear edged themselves along my spine.

"*Jannnnn . . . etttt!*" the wind whispered. "*Jannnn . . . etttt,*" came the pleading from the sea. My name was repeated over and over again.

I stood there by the open window, frozen in terror. Despite my fear, I wondered if those strange red lights were out there as they'd been the first time I heard the ghostly voice. The view from my window didn't encompass enough of the sea. I knew if I wanted to satisfy myself, I'd have to go to the lookout room.

I lit a lamp, turned its flame as high as it would go and quietly made my way to the stairs at the end of the corridor. I didn't want to waken Nancy. I was frightened enough as it was and I doubted she'd believe my story anyway, unless she actually heard the voice and saw the lights.

I reached the lookout room and stared out to sea, but there was nothing but darkness. I opened a window, my ears straining for the hollow sounds of my name, but the voice had ceased. I tried to comfort myself by insisting it had been only in my imagination, even the first time, but I was less than successful. To make doubly certain there was nothing out there, I extinguished the lamp.

Then I saw the small red lights bobbing up and down, as if they rested on the surface of the water. The sight of them was soon followed by more of those heartrending cries, as if coming from a soul in torment, calling out my name.

How could any living thing be out there in the middle of the night, I asked myself. What did the red lights mean? And who could it be, calling me by name, depending on the wind to carry the sound to me?

I was called a dozen more times until I wanted to cover my ears and shut out the sound. As suddenly, everything dissolved into silence and darkness. The red lights ceased to be and the wind died down so that all movement in the trees stopped and the surf's constant pounding was barely to be heard.

I knew then that I must have help with this weird situation. Certainly I couldn't call on Nancy. She'd say I was making it up, trying to frighten her out of the house. That was the last thing I wished to do, for I wondered if I could endure living here alone.

I had no friends in the village since my father's death, which meant I must place my trust in Jeff Cameron. I felt relieved once I made the decision and I relit the lamp, closed the window and moved silently back to my room.

I was in the corridor outside my bedroom when I heard a noise downstairs. It wasn't loud, it didn't consist of any creaks or groans from the flooring. It was more like a slight scratching noise, an unidentifiable sound. Yet all doors and windows were secure. I knew I'd be unable to sleep without investigating, so I reversed my steps and proceeded to the top of the stairs. Here I could look down into the reception hall, my lamplight creating a thousand flickering shadows on the ceilings and walls.

The sound was continuous. At the top of the stairs it was plainer, but still quite faint. There was nothing in this house I could associate with such a strange sound. I could hear no one moving about. Or was I wrong? Could Nancy have been awakened as I'd been? Was it she downstairs? The lack of a lighted lamp made me doubtful. I knew she was very superstitious and fearful of haunts. She always had been and she certainly wouldn't prowl without a lamp.

I went down the stairs, one step at a time. The sound never ceased. At the foot of the steps, I paused to try and locate the source. Now it seemed to be more of a scratching. Rather loud and apparently coming from the kitchen.

I passed the door to the cellar and moved on toward the kitchen. The sound, which had seemed to grow louder, now began to fade. I turned around and went back to the cellar door. That's where it seemed loudest.

I opened the door and knew at once the sound was coming from down there. It was stronger than ever. I shook my lamp slightly to move the supply of kerosene in the glass base. I didn't want the light to fail me down there where the darkness would be intense.

I descended half a dozen stairs when my courage began to fail me. I stood there, frozen in fear, while the noise

57

continued on and on. It appeared to originate at the very end of this spacious cellar, ceilinged with cobwebs and filled with everything from souvenirs a sailor brings home attesting to his travels around the world, to a massive anchor from a coastal steamer which Uncle Lew had once commanded before it blew up.

There were rows of old packing cases and barrels covering the earthen floor, all casting their eerie shadows. It required considerable will power for me to force myself to search out the source of the sound. I did, however, take the precaution of returning to the kitchen for another lamp. This one I left on the bottom steps so that if I dropped the lamp I carried, or it was blown out somehow, I'd have a beacon to guide me in the right direction. I could easily become lost in the vastness of this high-ceilinged cellar, if all light was denied me.

The very persistency of the sound now made me more annoyed than fearful. It wasn't a ghostly sound either, so I moved forward, trying to locate it. When I was near the north wall, I held my lamp higher to study the conglomeration of barrels and boxes haphazardly placed there. Hanging high above it all was the heavy anchor which my uncle had saved, perhaps for a sentimental reason. It was suspended from a rafter by means of a thick rope—probably the original ship's rope to which it had been attached while in service.

The sound came from below the anchor. Presently I realized it was confined to one of the big barrels and now it took on the form of the violent attempt of some animal to escape. Something was trapped inside the huge barrel and scampered about frantically.

I set the lamp down and pressed my ear against the side of the barrel. There was something alive inside it. I was no longer stricken by terror, for now I had a logical explanation for the sound.

I tried to move the barrel, but it wouldn't budge. Yet, when I rapped on it, there was a hollow reverberation, telling me it was empty. The scratching sounds ceased too, probably in fear. I knew whatever was in there must be set free, so I grasped the barrel and tugged. There seemed to be a rope tied to it, as if to hold it solidly against the wall.

I brought the lamp closer and saw that I was right, a rope was tied around the barrel and held by a slipknot, the easiest of all to untie. I gave the rope a hard pull, at the same time tugging at the barrel.

Everything seemed to happen in a fraction of a second. The barrel, untied, tilted in my direction so unexpectedly that I was thrown back, lost my balance and fell. As I hit the floor, the anchor came crashing down directly onto the barrel, which I'd been able to move only a matter of inches.

Staves flew about, some of them striking me with painful force. One of the barrel hoops somehow came free and rolled a few yards before toppling over.

Miraculously, my lamp, set on a nearby crate, wasn't knocked over. I scrambled to my feet, shaking badly from the fright of my brush with severe injury, or even death. The anchor weighed several hundred pounds and could have crushed me as easily as it had smashed the barrel.

I managed to hold the lamp higher and saw how the rope from which it had been suspended looked badly frayed at the point where it had broken. Because there was absolutely no reason why anyone would wish to kill me, I had to assume that this had been an accident. A strange one, perhaps, but still an accident.

I pried apart some of the staves and found a crushed and dead gray squirrel. The poor animal had been trapped inside and had made all that noise in an attempt to escape.

I heard footsteps on the floor above and some of the terror came back until I realized it was Nancy. She must have been awakened by the crash and was trying to locate its source.

"Nancy," I called out. The sound of my own voice helped restore some of my courage. Apparently it hadn't affected Nancy that way for she spoke my name in a voice that trembled with fright.

"It's all right," I called back. "I'm in the cellar. Something happened. Please come down."

She descended the stairs warily until the light of my lamp allowed her to identify me. She sidestepped the lamp still on the stairway and came quickly to my side. Her long flannel wrapper dragged in the dirt, but she paid no

59

heed to it. She stared at the smashed barrel, at the anchor imbedded in the debris and the earthen floor.

"I heard sounds," I explained. "I traced them down here and then to this barrel. I could hear some kind of animal inside it and I wanted to set it free. The barrel was lashed to the wall somehow. I slipped the knot and gave the barrel a yank. It came free when I didn't expect it to and I was thrown back. As this happened, the anchor rope broke and the anchor crashed down on the barrel. It was a squirrel trapped inside. The falling anchor killed it."

Nancy's breath all but whistled her relief. "I never realized how many strange sounds were in this house before Lew died. But at least this one has been explained. How in the world did that anchor come loose?"

I showed her, by lamplight, the frayed and now broken rope. "Well," she said, "it's been hanging there ever since I can remember. I told Lew more than once to get rid of it, or take it down, but he never got around to it. Drat all these things that are making this house so spooky."

I picked up the crushed little animal and placed it in a small box. Tomorrow I'd bury it out near the windbreak line of trees. I had a lamp in each hand as I went up the stairs behind Nancy. She closed the cellar door and went on to the kitchen where she promptly pushed the kettle from the back of the stove to the front and then stirred up the fire. In seconds the kettle was steaming.

She set out the tea, milk and sugar. We brewed it and sat down to recover from our experience.

"What I can't understand," I said, "is how the squirrel ever got into the barrel. I didn't see any signs of a hole in the sides and the top was covered."

"Those critters get in everywhere. Likely it dug a hole in the ground and the bottom of the barrel was open so it got in and then couldn't get out."

"Perhaps," I conceded, though I certainly wasn't sure. "I'm sorry you were awakened."

"Sleep later, that's all. Little to get up for any more. Not even the house is mine. Janet, are you thinking of selling the place?"

"Nancy, when I'm ready to leave here, I won't sell the house. I'll deed it to you free. That's a promise. I have no

60

use for it and you are certainly entitled to it."

"That's nice of you." She sipped her tea as complacently as if she'd expected to hear this. "No hurry, 'course."

"I won't leave for a while," I said, repressing a smile with difficulty. "Meantime, stop worrying about me selling the house. I assure you I won't."

"Thank you. If I had to leave, I don't know where I'd go, who I'd turn to."

I finished my tea and felt a return of sleepiness. I was still weak from the remnants of the terror I'd undergone. I wanted only to climb into bed and seek the release of all my fears through sleep. Once in bed, I left a lamp burning again, because the faint light did help to eliminate the darkness that brought fear.

In the morning I attended to the burial of the unfortunate squirrel. I also studied the wreckage of the barrel to try and determine if there had been some way for the animal to get inside. It was impossible to tell. After breakfast, I decided to walk along the beach, perhaps have another good look at the burned lifeboat. I intended to tell Jeff about that too.

It was a warm, beautiful day. The sea was calm, very blue, and there were scarcely any signs of white caps. I made up my mind to try my utmost to find out exactly what it was I'd seen out there on the bottom. In this quiet sea, and with the poplar to guide me, it wouldn't be difficult to locate the spot again.

I descended the stone stairs cut into the side of the bluff, made my way along the beach, now at low tide, until I came to the place where Uncle Lew had hidden the remains of the lifeboat. I was sure I had the right spot, but though I prodded the sand in all directions, there were no signs of the boat. After an hour's intensive search, I knew it had been taken away. A glance at the bush which had held the scrap of cloth revealed it was no longer there.

It was my fault because from the moment I'd come here, found the telltale piece of cloth and recognized its meaning, I'd given no heed to being spied upon until too late. I realized now I'd been observed—whether by someone on the water, or someone peering over the edge of the cliff, I knew not. Nor did it matter. Defeat flooded through me and with it came a return of fear. I realized I must work fast if I was to learn anything.

The disappearance of the remnants of the boat also indicated the necessity for not delaying the search of that wreck out at sea. I hurried along the beach to the boathouse where the dory was kept. I had another bathing suit there and I undressed quickly and donned it. I dragged the dory out to the edge of the water and then I searched the rocky beach for two good-sized, heavy stones. I placed these in the dory, shoved it into the water, scrambled aboard and began rowing.

There was no way I could conceal what I was doing now, but perhaps I could make it seem perfectly innocent if I was being watched. I didn't point the dory straight at the vicinity of the wreck, but well south of it and I gave the appearance of simply being out for a row.

After half an hour of this, I changed course and reached the spot where I could see the dim shadow of the hulk on the bottom. I threw out the sea anchor and then leaned back to lie down across the seat like someone idly enjoying being at sea.

I did nothing for about ten minutes. However, I dared not waste more time even though the sun was not very high yet. I picked up the two heavy stones, grasped them firmly, rolled over the side of the boat and let the weight of the stones drag me down.

I knew exactly how long I could hold my breath and there was a great deal to do in that very limited time. The stones pulled me all the way to the dark area and this time I could see it really was a wrecked vessel and not some large piece of flotsam, as I feared it might be.

I was able to roughly study the lines of the craft. I had never seen the ship which went down with my father, but this was a likely size for a private yacht. Then I saw something else, just before I knew I had to surface. There was a massive hole in the side of the hull—as if it had been the subject of an explosion.

My lungs were straining now so I planted my feet firmly on the edge of the wreck and gave myself a hard push upwards. I cleared the surface in moments and breathed in fresh air. I was tempted to go down again, but felt that was taking too much of a chance. This deep sea diving while alone was highly dangerous. Besides, if someone was watching, they might not be suspicious if I took just a brief swim. I might even be able to get aboard the dory without their being aware I'd slipped over the side.

I would have to provide some means of marking this spot however, though that could wait. I scrambled aboard the dory and lay down again for another ten minutes, resting and thinking about the hole ripped into the side of that ship.

Finally I sat up, pulled in the anchor, set the oars in the locks and rowed straight back to shore. At the boathouse I changed to my clothes and walked casually back to the house. When I came around to the front of the house, I saw Abner Pauley's horse and buggy tied there.

Much to my surprise, Nancy had set the dining room table. Obviously she believed it to be an occasion. Abner was bent over his plate, stuffing himself with cold lobster left from the night before. He was also enjoying a large green salad, plus biscuits and coffee. To one side, there was a huge serving of apple pie mounded with whipped cream. He made no attempt to rise when I entered the room, but he did nod a greeting.

Nancy, standing beside him to see that he lacked nothing in the way of food, motioned me to another chair. "There's plenty for you, Janet," she said, her manner surprisingly warm.

"No, thank you, Nancy," I replied. "I'll just have a cup of coffee."

She said, "Sit down. I'll bring it to you."

She looked like anything but a woman recently bereaved. Her eyes sparkled and it seemed as if she hated to leave Abner's side where she'd been standing to see, no doubt, that he lacked for nothing.

Abner finally stopped eating long enoough to speak. "Afternoon, Miss Janet. Really dropped by to talk to you again about selling."

I doubted that was his sole idea for the visit. Or was it? I wondered. Aloud, I said, "Mr. Pauley, I told you I did not wish to sell."

"So you did, but a woman often changes her mind. Believe me, I know, running a store where they want fancy beans and then it's regular beans, and then fancy again and finally they decide on squash. Never know a woman's mind, I do say."

"Then you'd better know mine, Mr. Pauley, or you'll be making a great number of trips here in vain. I will not sell under any circumstances."

He nodded, quite undaunted. "Keep askin' anyway. Talk's cheap. Come by to visit with Nancy. Now she's a widow, won't do to let her get lonely."

Abner Pauley had never in his lifetime worried about anyone's loneliness before. There was something afoot. It could be only that he'd had his eye on Nancy for some time and when Uncle Lew was killed decided it would be best to make an immediate approach. I could see that he was making headway too.

My aunt was not a good-looking woman and a smile on her face was a rarity. Her features were angualr, her lips thin and usually compressed tightly, as if in constant disapproval of everything about her. Yet today there was a softness to her mouth, a radiance in her eyes. She looked almost pretty. I couldn't help but feel a slight resentment that she was making no effort to hide her pleasure in having Abner here, though I was careful not to give any evidence of it. In all decency I believed she might have waited at least a month, out of respect to my uncle, before allowing the village tightwad to feel free to come here whenever he chose.

Also I was surprised that she hadn't told Abner I intended to sign the house over to her. I'd certainly ask her about it after he left. Just now I had a few questions of my own which I knew he'd be in a position to answer. There was little pertaining to anything that went on in these parts that he wasn't aware of. I wanted every bit of information I could get about the ship that had gone down with my father aboard.

"Mr. Pauley," I said, "how large was the yacht my father captained at the time of the sinking?"

"Tonnage? No idea, Miss Janet. None at all. Good size ship. Slept thirty passengers and the crew besides. She was called the *Cecelia,* after the owner's wife. Seen her only once. Didn't sail these waters often."

"Thank you."

"What'd you want to know for?" he asked.

"No reason beyond natural curiosity," I said. "Thank you again."

I excused myself and took my coffee to my room. Not long after I heard Abner leave. Nancy knocked on my door and came in at my invitation. She seemed flushed and rather excited. She was bursting with something to tell me.

"Janet, I've no right to ask this, but I have a mighty good reason to ask. How much longer will you be here?"

"Why do you wish to know?" I asked.

She actually giggled and her face suffused with color. "Guess I don't have to tell you. Way I been acting, anybody'd know. Ab Pauley's got his cap set for me. If he ain't, I've got mine set for him. I think he's going to ask me to marry him. He hinted all he wanted was this house for us to live in."

"Didn't you tell him I've promised you the house without cost?"

"No. Way I see, long as he thinks he can talk you into selling, he'll keep coming 'round."

"Then I won't tell him either. I do think you should wait a reasonable length of time, though. There'll be talk if you don't."

"Oh, he won't ask me right off. He's slow that way, but I can tell he's going to do it. 'Course I'll wait. Not too long though. You won't back down about the house?"

"Of course not. I'll stay a month or so. In that way, Abner can feel free to call because you're properly chaperoned, even if I should be out swimming or taking a stroll along the beach."

"You're a very good and thoughtful girl," Nancy said.

I did some serious thinking for a while after Nancy left my room. I couldn't reconcile myself to the idea of Abner's courting her so soon after my uncle's death. I also wondered if Abner might be using her. Yet why should he do such a thing?

How I wished Jeff would stop by. I felt it would be too

bold for me to seek him out, even though I wished to confide in him. Had I known him for a longer period, I'd have felt no compunction about going to him. But he was still a stranger. Yet I had to trust him. I needed advice.

I decided to change into something more feminine. He'd seen me only in serviceable clothes. I knew I should be wearing black for my uncle, but I'd ruined my only black dress the day after the funeral when I'd had that near-fatal fall at the cliff's edge.

I chose a walking dress, with blouse of pink velvet and a chestnut brown skirt trimmed with black gimp. I'd purchased it in Boston a few months ago and it was the latest in fashion. The pink highlighted my gray eyes and the little bows at the high neckline gave it a dainty, feminine look.

I dressed my hair with a fringe of curls on my brow, then drew it up to form a knot high on my head. I touched cologne to my ear lobes and felt quite elegant.

If Jeff came, it would be by boat. I knew he'd climb the bluff from the beach and so I decided to take a walk in that direction. If thinking of him would bring him here, he was already on his way. I left the house and reached the bluff just in time to see his lobster boat heading in toward the beach. He chose that moment to look up and I waved my arms frantically. He waved back and I went flying down those dangerous steps as if they were no more than the stairway in my home.

By the time I reached him, he had dragged the boat ashore.

"How lovely you look, Janet," he said, his glance admiring.

"Thank you," I replied. "I'm so grateful you came. I must talk with you."

"Has something happened?" he asked, sobering.

"A great deal," I replied. "And I would like to tell you about it. I'm sorely troubled and am desperately in need of a friend in whom to confide."

"You have one," he said, taking my arm and guiding me to a sandy area that was dry and protected from the sea breeze by large rocks. "Let's sit down here and talk."

He removed his jacket and spread it for me. I sat down,

using a rock to support my back. He sat alongside me, his back against the same rock.

Without further ado, I began. "You know the story of my father going down with his ship. I mean, the story the public knows. You know, too, that my uncle was supposed to have further blackened the family name by meeting death in a less-than-gentlemanly fashion."

"You know what I think of that," he said.

I nodded. "Now I am going to tell you of a secret letter my uncle left me. A letter which no one but myself read."

"Do you have it?" he asked.

"No," I replied. "His instructions were that I destroy it after reading and absorbing its contents. I did."

Jeff looked as if he didn't approve of that, but all he said was, "Please continue."

"It will take a while, so I beg of you to be patient and I hope you will believe everything I say."

"Be assured I will," he said.

"I hope so, though I fear some of it will tax your credulity," I replied and began my story.

I told him of finding the letter in the secret compartment of my uncle's desk. I recited the letter almost verbatim, for its contents were burned into my memory. I told him of hearing my name called and how it sounded as if it were coming from the depths of the sea, of seeing the small red lights bobbing on the water. Of hearing footsteps in the house later that night and, after hearing the front door close, coming down to investigate, finding wet, sandy footprints on the veranda. Of discovering the burned hull of a lifeboat buried nearby—a lifeboat bearing the name *Cecelia*.

I spoke of being awakened again last night by the sound of my name being called and seeing the lights at sea. Then, while returning to my room from my uncle's lookout room, of hearing the noise in the basement and, in seeking out its source, I was nearly killed by the anchor. I told him of my discovery of the wreck of a boat out at the spot where we'd become acquainted yesterday. Through all of it Jeff remained silent, yet his somber mien revealed his interest and concern.

When I finished, he whistled softly. "That's quite a story."

"I know it is, Jeff, but do you believe it?"

"Every word," he assured me. "And now I will you tell you something I couldn't until you took me into your confidence. You see, though I knew your uncle but briefly, I believe he was about to take me into his confidence. But he was killed before he could do so."

"Did he tell you any of what I did?" I asked.

"Not a word," Jeff admitted, "except that he was of the opinion that the wreck could well have occurred in these parts."

"Why didn't you inform me of that?"

"I tried to gain your confidence," he chided me mildly. "You weren't ready to trust me."

"True," I admitted. "And to be even more frank, I fear only desperation has caused me to do so. After last night, I felt I could no longer cope with the mystery of what was happening by myself."

"Will you show me where the burned remains of the lifeboat are buried?"

"I'll show you where it *was* buried. Someone apparently observed me uncovering it and they took it elsewhere. "When I went to check on it today, it was gone."

"How did you find it" he asked.

"My uncle had left a clue by placing a bit of canvas on a sturdy limb of a branch that indicated its location," I said. "He didn't say so in the letter, but the moment I saw it, I surmised its meaning."

"Then I'd say you were under close observation and no doubt in danger," he said thoughtfully.

"Do you really believe that, Jeff?" I asked.

"Yes," he said.

"In that case, perhaps you are also," I said. "Since you were seen in my uncle's company the week of his death."

"I scarcely think so," Jeff said. "After all, I'm nothing but a lobsterman. I couldn't know much. And who in the village, that your uncle tried to convince, believed in your father's innocence?"

"No one," I said promptly.

"What does your aunt say about all this?"

"She knows very little of what I've told you," I replied.

"How little?" he asked.

"She knows about someone having been in the house. I told her of the wet, sandy footsteps on the porch. She wouldn't believe it, saying I was trying to frighten her into leaving the house. She's superstitious and believes in haunts."

"She must have heard the disturbance in the cellar last night," Jeff reasoned.

"Yes," I replied. "She was awakened by the crash of the anchor and came down to investigate. I never told her about hearing my name called or the lights that bobbed on the water."

"Why not?" he asked.

"The day we returned here after my uncle's funeral, I took a walk to the cliff. I was preoccupied with dismal thoughts and became careless. When I noticed the fog closing in again, I turned to go back to the house and slipped on the wet grass. I fell and nearly went over."

I shuddered at the memory. He reached over and took one of my hands in his. "Go on," he said.

"When I returned to the house and Nancy saw my dress all muddied, she asked me what had happened. When I told her, she said that proved that Uncle Lew's death was an accident. I reminded her he never went near the bluff when it was foggy. That I'd been foolish to do so. She agreed as to my foolishness, adding that I'd perhaps not fallen at all. That it would have been a simple matter to muddy my dress to make it appear I'd had a fall."

"I gather she doesn't particularly care about you," he said.

"She didn't at the moment," I said. "She'd just learned my uncle's will left the house to me."

"The more you tell me, the more fearful I become of your safety," he said. "Will you take me to the house and show me the barrel that imprisoned the squirrel?"

"You may inspect all there's left of it. The barrel was somehow lashed to the wall. The rope was held by only a slip knot. I was trying to tip the barrel over to let the squirrel out so I slipped the knot. When I tugged on the barrel again, it moved so unexpectedly I was thrown back. Most fortunately, because there was a heavy anchor hanging from a rope right above it, and the rope broke at that very moment. The anchor fell on the barrel and the squirrel was crushed to death."

"It could have been planned," Jeff reasoned. "It could well be you were lured down there by the noise the trapped squirrel made. When you attempted to release the poor animal, the anchor was to fall and kill you."

"I'll admit I've been frightened by these various things I've told you about, but I must also state that the rope holding the anchor was badly frayed."

"But did you touch it? Place the slightest pressure on it?"

"Absolutely none."

"I want to see that rope. First though, show me where the lifeboat was buried."

He helped me to my feet, shook the sand from his jacket and we walked down to where I'd uncovered the burned prow of the lifeboat. Jeff prodded the area with a stick. Satisfied there was no longer any trace of it, he tossed it away and we headed for the steps cut into the side of the cliff.

FIVE

On our way to the house, I told Jeff about Abner's visit to my aunt and how he had again pressed me to sell him the house.

"Did he say why he wanted it?" Jeff asked.

"No," I replied with a smile. "But Nancy is convinced he's going to propose to her and he hinted he wanted the house for them to live in."

"Her husband hasn't been dead a week," Jeff exclaimed, aghast at the idea.

"I know, and at first I was as stunned as you are now," I told him. "I have a feeling that Abner is using Nancy. If I'm right, he's making a fool of her. I resent his doing so."

Jeff looked thoughtful. "I wonder if he could know something we don't."

"If he does, I can't imagine what it is," I replied. "However, Nancy has a little secret also. I told her that when I left here—which I intend to do shortly—I am going to deed the house to her without cost. She didn't pass that information on to Abner, for fear he might cease his visits."

"Humph," was all Jeff said, for we'd reached the house and there was no time for further discussion.

Nancy met us inside. She seemed pleased to see Jeff until I explained the reason for his visit.

"I do think you're making far too much of what happened last night," she said coldly.

"I could have been killed," I said.

"You could have been killed when you fell near the cliff two days ago," she retorted. "At least, you said you fell.

71

No one saw you. No one saw the anchor fall on you last night."

"Why would I lie?" I asked, more hurt than angry.

"To frighten me into leaving this house," she retorted.

"I already told you I was going to deed it to you."

"You've done nothing about putting it in writing though," she argued.

"I see no need for it," I said. "I've never lied to you."

"I think you're given to telling fanciful tales," she said. "And I think it's for just one reason—to frighten me."

"Nancy, this is very embarrassing for Jeff."

"I'm glad he's here," she said, completely unmollified. "I'm glad I have a witness to what you're trying to do to me."

"I'm sure Janet has no wish to frighten you, or drive you from this house," Jeff said, his manner stern. "I've known her but two days, but it was quite obvious to me from the first that she is a young woman of sterling character."

"So she's turned you against me," she said scornfully. "Very well. I'll say no more. But if anything happens to me, I hope the village constable will have sense enough to investigate my death."

I was so aghast at her words, I could only shake my head in disbelief. Jeff placed a protective arm about my waist, as if by doing so he could shut out the ugliness of what she'd insinuated. I closed my eyes, forcing back tears which threatened to come. I could hear the clomp-clomp of my aunt ascending the stairs, followed by the slam of her bedroom door.

"That was a horrible thing for her to say. Her resentment toward you is very apparent. Why don't you leave this place now? You can't change anything by staying here. Deed the house over to her if you wish, but get away from here. I'm fearful for your safety."

"I can't," I said, still shaken, though comforted by his nearness. "My uncle left me this house so that I'd have the opportunity to find out what he couldn't. I won't abandon my search. If you wish to continue working with me, I'll be grateful. Otherwise I must carry on alone."

"Then take me to the cellar," he said, releasing me. "I want to see if I can determine exactly what happened."

72

I led him to the kitchen where I lit two lamps, handed him one. Even by day, the cellar was a dismal, shadowy place. Downstairs, we approached the scene where the smashed barrel lay.

Jeff examined it. "Too broken up to tell if there was a hole in it large enough for a squirrel to get through, but we're not going to pass by the idea that the squirrel was sealed in the barrel so it would make a great deal of noise and bring you down here to investigate." Jeff rolled another barrel over so he could stand on it and look at the remnants of rope hanging from the rafter. He jumped down and examined the end of the rope still tied to the anchor itself.

He looked up at me. "Didn't you say the barrel was lashed to the wall?"

"I'm really not sure. It was tied to something because there was a rope around it with that slipknot I told you about."

"This rope does seem frayed," he observed, "but it could have been weakened by rubbing something abrasive against it to a point where it would break when the full weight of the anchor was put on it."

"The weight was on it," I said. "The anchor hung free."

"I wonder. There are these peices of rope here and I can't figure out what they're for exactly, but I'm puzzled as to why an empty barrel should have been lashed to the wall. You notice there's a metal ring screwed into the wall directly behind where the barrel must have been." He maneuvered around the fallen anchor and bent low to study the area.

"The rope could have been tied around the barrel, looped through this ring, followed upwards to one of the rafters, led on over it and then tied to the lower part of the rope holding up the anchor to take up most of the weight. A series of slipknots would have done it. You tried to move the barrel, found it lashed. You pulled the slipknot down here, the second rope fastened below the frayed one was really supporting the anchor's weight. When you loosened it, the weight pulled the rope, slipped another knot and the full weight was suddenly placed on the

73

frayed portion. It gave way as it was planned to do, and the anchor fell. It was meant to crush anyone who freed the barrel."

He pulled the ropes free and showed me where the second one had been tied to the rope below the broken part. I brought my hands up to my face and, despite myself, I burst into tears. The knowledge that someone had actually attempted to murder me was almost more than I could bear. Jeff's arms enclosed me tenderly.

"They failed that time and there won't be any others," he vowed. "I'm going to stay near this house all night long and during the day as much as possible."

"Oh, Jeff, you can't! There are your lobster traps. . . ."

"They can wait. My sole interest now is keeping you alive. Someone wants to kill you. I don't know why, but it must be connected with your father's ship. We've got to find out what this is all about—and soon. Before something else happens."

"Jeff, I'm sure I found the wreck. At least I think it's the wreck. I dived down to it this morning. It looks to me as if there's a great hole blown through the side of the ship."

His voice was grimmer than I'd ever heard it. "I've thought it possible the ship was deliberately sunk. I believed your uncle thought so too. I even suggested it to him, but we never could come up with any good reason."

"What can we do?" I asked.

"Take every precaution. If you hear any sounds, see anything, call out. From now on I'll be close by the house. I want to see those lights too, hear that voice calling your name."

"It's so awful to hear!" I shuddered. "It sounds like someone in terrible anguish, calling to me as the only person who can save him. Though it has hollow sound, it's a man's voice. I even thought it was my father's."

"You're supposed to think it's your father's voice. The lights I don't understand. So far as I know, it's not possible for anyone to work below the surface of the sea in darkness. There's no light yet known that will shine under water. You'd have to seal the flame inside something and there'd be no oxygen to keep the flame burning. The lights cannot have anything to do with diving to the wreck, if that's what's going on out there."

"I'm not certain it comes from the area directly above the wreck."

"You must let me know when the lights and voice return."

"Tonight I'll go to the widow's walk and wait. If I hear them, I'll call down to you. I'll show you how to reach the walk now."

I took him to the lookout room and showed him the ladder leading to the walk, which was reached through a trap door.

"I'll be outside," he vowed. "Depend on it. Just now, I suggest we take another look at the wreck. It's early afternoon. The light ought to be sufficient."

"A good idea," I exclaimed.

Jeff glanced out the window. "There goes Nancy. I wonder what's on her mind?"

"I don't know." I was equally puzzled as I watched her move along the road. "She's obviously going to the village. Do you suppose she's gone to talk with Abner—I mean, about the ugly suspicions she has in her mind regarding me?"

"Let's not concern ourselves about it," Jeff suggested wisely. "We have more important things to do. We'll row out to the wreck in my boat. Sorry I don't have a bathing suit with me."

"I'll change to mine," I told him. "While you're waiting, you can gather up some heavy stones and put them in the boat. I'll need them for weights."

I went directly to the boathouse, leaving Jeff to hunt a supply of large rocks.

"We'd better put a marker out there," he advised, "or you might not find the spot too quickly. We can tie one of my lobster traps to a long line. If you reach the wreck, you can attach the line and pull the trap well under the water where it won't be readily seen except by us. The trap is freshly painted red, so you can pull it down to quite a depth."

I ran to the dory shed where I had one of my bathing suits. I changed into it and rejoined Jeff. We pushed the craft into deeper water and he manned the oars. I watched the poplar tree and gave him directions. We were fortunate in finding the wreck quickly and I could once again see that dim, barely visible object below.

"First," I said, "we'd better mark it." I tied one end of the thin rope to my wrist while Jeff tied the other end to one of his traps. He threw this overside. I seized two stones, rolled out of the boat and let the stones carry me down. I reached the hulk, but I didn't take time to examine it. I found a projecting piece of wood, dropped the rocks and tied the lobster trap line to it. Then I pulled until I could look up and see the red trap above me, but well under water.

My lungs were aching so I kicked myself to the surface and breathed hard for a few minutes while I clung to the side of the boat.

"Looks good down there." Jeff indicated the lobster trap. "We can now find the wreck without wasting time. Do you feel strong enough to go down again?"

"I could go down half a dozen more times," I said. "This time I'm going to have a good look. The sunlight is fine down there, Jeff. Hand me two of those rocks, please."

I gripped the side of the boat with my elbows, took the rocks Jeff offered, released my hold and went down.

I followed the rope line to the hulk, swam to the prow. I saw the lettering. It was faded but discernible. The name painted on the prow was the *Celtic*. We had the wrong ship! I'd never felt so utterly frustrated in my life.

I fought my way to the surface and had to swim to the boat Jeff helped me aboard. I panted out the news.

"Are you sure?" he asked. "*Cecelia* and *Celtic* are so much the same."

"Positive," I replied, feeling utterly defeated. "There was sufficient light to see by."

"Don't be too discouraged. I'll look into this. Have any other ships been reported lost around here in the last few years?"

"None that I know of," I said gloomily. "Not even Papa's ship was known to have gone down in this area."

"The hulk isn't decayed?"

"No . . . there's only that awful hole in her side."

"Then she went down about the time your father's ship sank. Someone should know about it."

"Can you find out?"

"Yes. Finchport, just up the coast, has a telegraph office. I'll have word sometime tomorrow. Thank heavens, in this day and age, we have the speed of the telegraph to help us. Soon as I return, I'll begin patrolling around your house. You may not see me, but I'll be there."

"It will make me feel much better," I said. "Provided you're in no danger."

"I'll be cautious. Don't worry. Let's get back. I'll go directly to the telegraph office."

He rowed rapidly and I jumped overboard before we reached shallow water, to swim the rest of the way. At the boathouse, I changed. I couldn't shake off the glum feeling of disappointment at learning the submerged wreck was the *Celtic* rather than the *Cecelia*.

I used the steps leading to the top of the bluff, dreading my return to the house. I was stunned at Nancy's behavior because I felt we had reached a rapport earlier in my room. Could it be that Abner had sowed the seeds of poison in her mind in regard to me? Had she gone to consult him? I wondered what her manner would be when she returned.

I didn't have long to wait. From the window of my bedroom I saw her coming up the road. Rather than have harsh words in this room, I decided to go downstairs. Though the thought of further disharmony between us sorely distressed me, I knew I had to face it. Furthermore, it had suddenly occurred to me I hadn't eaten since breakfast, and I was ravenous.

We met in the downstairs hall. Nancy slipped the shawl from her shoulders, loosened her bonnet and hung them on the wall rack.

"Will you please light the fireplace in the parlor, Janet?" she asked. "My bones ache and it's as good a place to talk as any."

"Certainly." I followed her into the room and she took her usual chair to one side of the hearth. I lit the fire and gave my attention to it for a few minutes, using the

77

bellows to help the flames catch more quickly. That done, I sat down opposite her.

She rocked a while, regarding me silently. When I could no longer endure it, I said, "What is it, Nancy?"

"I've been to see Abner," she said. "I went to him for advice. About you."

"I suppose you told him I was trying to frighten you out of this house," I said wearily, knowing now what was coming.

"I did," she stated belligerently. "I also told him I believe you made that anchor fall yourself. He agrees with me. He's worried you're trying to do me in."

"Why would I?" I countered. "I'm going to give you this house."

"I don't believe it," she retorted, ceasing her rocking to lean forward as if to emphasize the importance of what she was about to say. "But I'll tell you what I do believe and Abner agrees. I believe you're going to kill me so you can get all my wealth . . . and it's considerable."

"I know it is, Nancy," I said. "But I want no part of it. I have a comfortable sum in the bank which Papa left me."

"Nothing like what I've got," she snapped.

"No," I agreed. "But sufficient for my needs."

"I also told Abner you're conspiring with that young man against me," she said.

"Nancy, I'm afraid you're losing your mind," I said, thoroughly annoyed at her foolishness.

Her arm extended and she pointed a bony finger at me. "Now you're saying I'm insane!"

"Do you blame me, when you start making statements like that?"

"Abner says I should get out of here, that I'm not safe in this house."

"Why don't you?" I asked with a sigh. "If you're afraid that I want to do you in because I want your money."

"So you admit it," she said, her voice triumphant.

"I admit no such thing," I replied, my patience fast ebbing. "But I think you're foolish to stay here when you're afraid of me. If I were fearful you wished to kill me, I'd get out."

"I'd never do anything to you," she said, giving me a disdainful look.

"I know it," I said quietly. "Nor will I harm you."

"I'm not so sure," she said. "But I'll tell you one thing—I'm not getting out of here. No matter what you do to try to frighten me out of my wits and my sanity."

I could endure no more of this ugly, foolish talk. "I'm hungry, Nancy. I'll prepare supper if you'll tell me what you want."

"I'll do the cooking in this house," she said, rising. "You'll get no chance to poison me."

I restrained the smile which almost touched my lips. "Do you mind if I eat with you?"

"No," she said. "I feel safer with my eye on you."

I arose. "I'll set the table."

"We'll eat in the kitchen," she said, her tone daring me to suggest otherwise.

"I expected we would." And this time I did smile, for I was thinking of the special service and attention Abner got.

"I know you're laughing at Abner. But he's been mighty good to me. I now get all my groceries at cost. After we're married, I'll get them free."

"Has he proposed?" I asked, as I followed her to the kitchen.

"No," she replied, "but he will."

I attended to my chore of setting the table. She moved capably about the kitchen, mixing dumplings for the fricasee chicken which simmered on the back of the stove. She was an excellent cook and the fragrance emanating from the pot was tantalizing.

I did enjoy it, though supper was a silent affair. I was glad I wasn't fearful of Nancy trying to do me in, for had there been a poisonous brew in the chicken, I'd never have survived it. I couldn't resist a second portion and though Nancy didn't know, I'd caught the glance of satisfaction she cast my way as I reached for the platter.

But the breach of suspicion between us had widened

and I gave up all hope of ever bridging it.

After dinner, I suggested I wash and dry the dishes, but my services were refused. I went up to the lookout room to watch for Jeff, hopeful he would return before dark. I knew he would remain here on guard and I knew I would sleep better tonight, knowing he was on the premises.

I sat in my uncle's chair, once again filled with the discouragement that had overcome me when the hulk I'd discovered on the ocean bottom was not that of Papa's ship. I'd been so sure, yet I had no real reason to be. Except that so many things seemed to be happening all around me and directed at me, that I had begun to assume I was the victim of a planned scheme meant to do me harm because I was investigating the wreck. Now it seemed that I was wrong.

I suddenly recalled Uncle Lew's book of ship registrations. I jumped up and rapidly scanned the volumes on the wall shelves. Sure enough, there it was a recognized authority on all ships afloat. I quickly discovered the Celtic. It was a yacht of Boston manufacture. That certainly seemed like a description of the ship I'd found on the bottom. I looked for the registry of the Cecelia, but it wasn't listed. The register was forty years old so perhaps the Cecelia hadn't been built in time to be among the ships described.

I'd been so engrossed in my find that I'd forgotten to watch for Jeff. But a hasty glance in the direction of the bluff revealed him moving briskly toward the house. I closed the book, fled down the two flights of stairs and was on the porch just as he reached it.

Without a word we went into each other's arms and his lips touched mine. It was a gentle embrace, yet one filled with meaning. When I entered the shelter of his arms, I felt love for this man I'd known only two days flood through me. The gentle way he held me told me better than words I was very special to him . . . as I wanted to be.

"I missed you," he said when he released me.

"And I you," I replied, knowing full well the emotion I felt was revealed in my face and my voice. "Come inside. Have you eaten?"

"I didn't take the time," he replied. "As for going inside, what about your aunt?"

"I doubt she'll bother you," I said. "She's still sulking. As for being welcome, you are. The house is mine."

"So it is," he said with a grin. "In that case, I'll accept your invitation for a little food."

"Good." As we passed through the reception hall on our way to the kitchen, I heard an upstairs door slam. Jeff and I exchanged knowing grins.

"At least, we'll have privacy," I said. "I want to tell you about a discovery I made while you were gone."

In the kitchen I set about frying chicken, plus skillet fried potatoes. I warmed green beans and prepared a salad. For dessert, I served berry pie and coffee. While I prepared the food, I told Jeff about checking the *Celtic* in Uncle Lew's ship registry. "That's the *Celtic* down there. It answers perfectly to the description."

"That's a disappointment," Jeff said, sobering. "It destroys your uncle's theories and ours also. In any case, I telegraphed New York for information about the *Cecelia* and the *Celtic*. I should get an answer tomorrow."

"Of course, we must bear in mind the fact that no one saw the *Cecelia* out there that night. Our only evidence that she could have been lies in the discovery of the lifeboat, and that could have drifted ashore from somewhere much farther out."

"True enough," Jeff conceded. "But there's this to consider. The *Cecelia* was on her way to a point just north of here and she'd have been following the coastline. I think that if anyone aboard that ship caused it to sink, they'd have done so when they were as close to land as possible. It's no fun bobbing around in a lifeboat a hundred miles at sea."

"All we can do is wait," I said. "Of course if that is not the ship we're searching for, the strange things that occurred were either coincidence or . . . there's some other reason why my presence is not wanted here."

"I can tell you this: it wasn't coincidence. I took along some of that frayed rope and looked at it under a glass. It had been filed. You could see the little particles of metal filings which must have clung to the tool before it

81

was used on the rope. The anchor was either meant to fall on you, or scare you to death."

"So far as scaring me, it certainly accomplished its purpose," I said. "Did you notice there's no moon tonight? And very little starlight. It's a good night for someone to be out there with the red lights, calling my name."

"I thought of that. Remember, I'll be very close by and the boat is ready to be shoved into the water. I've even provided it with two sets in the expectation that my passenger this evening won't be averse to a little rowing—so we can get out there as quickly as possible."

"I'll risk blisters if it will do any good," I told him. "I still want to know who's trying to frighten me and why."

"So do I," he said, attacking the plate I set before him with gusto. "I want to get this business over with as quickly as possible for two reasons. First, I want to get you away from here. Not only for your own safety, but I don't like the way you've been treated. The second reason should really come first. I'm more than fond of you, Janet. I believe you know that. Your loveliness touched my heart from the moment you turned around in church and our eyes met."

"Thank you, Jeff." I know my smile was wistful. "You have no idea the gap of loneliness you've filled in my life. It's a frightening feeling—loneliness. I never knew it while my parents were alive. Except when Papa went off to sea. While Mama was living, we always voyaged with Papa. Whatever ship he captained was our home. I had a very exciting childhood. Then, after Papa died, I had Uncle Lew. Nancy tolerated me until after my uncle's death. On our way to the funeral, she asked me how soon I'd leave. Of course, when we returned and she learned Uncle Lew had left the house to me, she couldn't order me from it. For a little while I thought we could be friends. Now I realize that will never be."

"If your uncle hadn't left you the house, would you have left immediately?"

"I doubt I'd have had any choice," I said, refilling his cup with hot coffee and pouring some for myself. "Yes, I believe I'd have gone to Boston. You see, though I suspected my uncle's death was other than an accident, I

82

could think of no motive. Even though the villagers avoided him as they did me, that was because of Papa."

"When you leave here, I hope you'll choose New York instead of Boston," he said with a smile.

"Why?" I asked.

"Because that's where I come from," he said.

"Who are you really?" I asked. "While I don't believe you've been dishonest with me, I have a feeling you've been evasive."

One corner of his mouth quirked up in an embarrassed smile. "Perhaps. But it's true that I'm making a little extra money lobstering. Does that satisfy you?"

"I guess for the time being it will have to," I said with a smile. I still felt he was holding back.

"I think I'm going to have to propose to you," he said, taking a final sip of coffee. "You're an excellent cook."

"I can't take credit for much of it," I said. "It's Nancy who excels in the kitchen, though I enjoy preparing food."

I arose and started to clear the table, refusing Jeff's help.

"In that case," he said, "I'm going outside to keep a lookout. Lock the kitchen door, but leave the front door unlocked, for my convenience. You'll not be in danger. I'll keep it in view all the time. I'd like you to keep a watch in the lookout room. If you see any lights, call to me. I'll come flying up the stairs. I want to see them."

"I'll do that," I said. "I'd feel better if someone other than I saw them."

"Better leave a lamp on in the hall so I'll be able to find my way," he said. "In case I come rushing in."

I nodded. "I'll go up there as soon as I've finished my kitchen chores."

"Good girl." He again took me in his arms, kissed me briefly and went out the kitchen door. I locked it behind him, turned to my dishes and straightened up the kitchen.

I extinguished the lamps, except for one which I carried with me. The only lamp glowing in the front of the house was the one on the hall table. Obviously Nancy had no intention of coming downstairs again.

I carried my lamp upstairs and went to my room, but I didn't remain there very long. I made my way quietly to the lookout room and before I reached the top of the stairs to open the door, I extinguished the lamp.

It was eerie, sitting up there alone, in darkness. I could hear the surf but I couldn't see the ocean. I had no idea of passing time because I seemed to be in a dark, private and timeless world of my own. I kept my eyes turned toward the sea, waiting for the lights, listening for the voice.

A breeze began stirring the trees. I grew more apprehensive and I found myself leaning forward in the direction of the sea. Then, suddenly, the lights appeared. Not as if someone had just lit them, but as if they'd been raised out of the sea itself, already glowing with that weird red light.

I opened the windows to listen. When I heard no cry, I clambered up the ladder to the widow's walk. I leaned over the railing and spoke Jeff's name. I heard him call back in a soft voice. Then came the melancholy voice. With the regularity of a foghorn, the call was repeated over and over. The red lights were still there.

The next moment they vanished and the calling voice ceased, only seconds before Jeff arrived, breathing quickly from his haste.

I needed his presence. My fear was overwhelming tonight. I clung to him and I told him about the lights and the voice. "Just before you got here it stopped. Jeff, it's almost as if they—or whatever it is—knew you were here."

"Let's get out there and see if we can find anything."

We left the house silently so as not to waken Nancy. Clear of the house we ran, hand in hand. We made our cautious way down the bluff stairs, finding each step by feeling for it. Jeff led and kept a protective grip about my waist.

His boat was ready. I manned one set of oars, he the other and we rowed very fast, with all our combined strength.

I could barely make out the faint outline of the poplar rising nakedly from the top of the bluff and silhouetted dimly. We reached the approximate position of the wreck and began circling about. We rowed for an hour but observed nothing. Finally we both sagged over the oars. I was exhausted and our efforts had all been in vain.

Tired as I was, a thought came to me. "Jeff, if that's the hulk of the *Celtic* out here, where did the lifeboat from the *Cecelia* come from?"

"Perhaps I can give you the answer to that tomorrow. Let's go back. There's nothing out here."

"I don't like the way the calling voice and bobbing lights stopped just as you were in a position to bear out my story," I said worriedly. "I don't understand it. How could anyone out here know you were guarding my house? It's as if they're trying to show me up in your eyes as a liar, or a simpleton."

"I believe you, my dear," he said. "I do wish I'd heard the voice and seen the lights. But if they did it tonight, they'll do it again. The next time I might be luckier."

"You said 'if'," I said. "Don't you really believe me?"

"I really do, Janet Vance," he said and the firmness of his tone assured me he meant it.

SIX

Late the following morning I heard the clomp-clomp of horses' hoofs coming up the driveway. Nancy also heard their approach and came from the kitchen, walking quickly to the door. When she opened it, a resplendent carriage containing three passengers had already stopped and the driver, a handsome young man of no more than twenty-three or four, was assisting a beautiful young lady to alight. She was followed by a white-haired, portly gentleman who wore a tan coat and trousers, a plaid waistcoat from which a thick gold watch chain dangled. He carried a gold-headed cane and he appeared very suave, very self-assured.

As they approached the veranda, I couldn't help but note how fashionably the young woman was dressed. Her summer tweed coat and skirt was the latest in fashion. The revers of the coat were faced with black moiré; the skirt lined with scarlet silk. She had a peaches-and-cream complexion and golden hair complemented by a straw hat trimmed with marguerites. The young man, I might add, was almost foppishly dressed. His morning coat and striped trousers seemed strangely out of place in a village populated mostly by fishermen.

Nevertheless, it was pleasant to see such elegant strangers and I know Nancy was as curious as I to learn the purpose of their visit.

The white-haired man removed his hat and presented us with a courtly bow. "Ladies, I am at your service. My name is Michael Yates, from Boston, madam, miss. This is my daughter Daphne and my secretary Mr. Roy Lacey."

86

Nancy was overawed to the point of speechlessness, so I did the honors.

"Good morning," I said. "I am Miss Janet Vance and this is my aunt, Mrs. Lewis Vance."

He bowed again. His secretary bowed and his daughter stood by, smiling warmly.

"Won't you come in?" I invited.

"At a later date, we'll accept your gracious invitation with enthusiasm. This is merely a brief visit to acquaint you with our business in these parts. I am a promoter, Miss Vance. I build hotels, get them started and sell them at a profit. I have come today to inquire concerning your interest in selling this piece of property. I assure you I will pay a high price for it."

"A pity you didn't write me, sir, and have thus saved yourself time and expense, for the property is not for sale."

"Ah, but you haven't heard my offer, Miss Vance. Nor do you realize that everything changes in time. This is an old house. It should be replaced in the interest of bettering the community. The hotel I would build here will attract four or five thousand people each season. Good spenders, all of them, or they wouldn't pay the prices I charge. These kind of people bring money to your village. There isn't a person in that little town who won't prosper if the hotel comes into being."

"The answer is no," I reiterated. "No doubt all you say is quite true, but I'm not interested."

"Well, I'm disappointed, I must say. May I call some evening soon to discuss this further? I might convince you to change your mind. Besides, after coming all this distance, don't you believe I should have a chance to at least make my offer?"

Before I could reply, Nancy said, "Come for supper tomorrow night. We'll be honored to have you."

I was annoyed, but common courtesy prevented me from showing it.

The girl approached me with a warm smile. "I hope you and I can be friends," she said, apparently sensing my displeasure.

"Thank you," I replied. "I hope so too."

I accepted her hand extended in a gesture of friendship. Just as I withdrew mine, Michael Yates captured it and bowed, murmuring his gratitude at being asked to supper. I didn't bother to remind him the idea wasn't mine. We watched as they returned to their carriage, seated themselves. Mr. Lacey urged the horses into action and, with a farewell wave, they drove off.

Nancy motioned to the rockers decorating the front of the porch. "Sit down, Janet."

I looked at her in surprise. "Not for another argument, I hope."

"No," she said briskly. "I was just thinking that if the place was mine, I'd sell. No reason why you can't turn it over to me now, is there? You could stay as long as you liked."

"Really, Nancy, you do surprise me."

"No reason why I should," she said. She was rocking rapidly and I couldn't help but think her mind was as busy as the rocker. "It's true. This house is old. Cellar's full of junk. Whole place is."

"There are some very valuable things in this house. There are linens and furniture and lamps from all over the world."

"Oh, I'd sell those. Get a pretty penny for them too. Abner and I—after we're married—are aimin' to travel. In real style, I might add."

"You've discussed it?" I asked, no longer stunned at any statement she made.

"Not a word," she admitted glibly. "But we will. I'm already makin' plans. He'll go along. He's got quite a case on me, in case you don't know."

"I'm becoming more and more aware of it," I said. "I only hope you won't let him take advantage of you. You're quite an innocent woman, you know."

She sniffed. "The man ain't born who could fool me."

"I hope not, for your sake."

"If you weren't so much younger'n me, I'd swear you were jealous," she said, her laughter a cackling sound.

I smiled. "Nancy, I wish we could be friends."

The rocking ceased and she cocked her head to study me more carefully. "Sometimes I think you mean it. Other times I think you're scheming to drive me outa here. But you're not going to do it. Abner told me to watch out for you."

"And I'm telling you to watch out for Abner."

"I'm not going to sit here and listen to you down a good man," she said indignantly. "Thought I could appeal to your generous nature, but you're as stingy as your uncle was."

"When you make such a statement, it's difficult for me to believe you ever loved him.."

"I never said I did," she retorted boldly.

"Then I'll say something more. I hope you do marry Abner. I think you and he deserve each other."

"It'll be a good marriage," she said with a defiant nod. "You wait and see. You'll be here, 'cause you're never going to deed me this house."

"Yes, I am, Nancy," I replied with a sigh. "But not until I'm ready. I'm not even sure you're capable of managing your affairs."

"Now you're saying I'm crazy," she shrilled. "You want to have me put away, but you won't. Abner won't let you."

"I'm not, Nancy," I argued. "But you know Abner's reputation for greed as well as I. It's my fear that it's your money he's after.

"He has plenty of his own," she blurted. "It's you who's after my money. You'd get everything if I went over that cliff the way your uncle did. You're the only one left to get my money. First you try to frighten me to death by making up weird stories. But that didn't work, so now you're trying to tell me I'm crazy in the head."

"Oh, please, Nancy, I don't wish to discuss it further."

"I don't either," she said rising. "And I don't care if you never leave me the house. If you don't get out of here soon, I'm going to. I can live with Abner's sister. That was his idea too. He even told me I'd be safer there. Safer from you."

I sighed in discouragement as she went into the house, and decided to go down to the beach for a stroll. The pounding of the surf had always had a soothing effect on me. I used the cliff steps, moving cautiously. I was so engrossed in my thoughts that I didn't even see Jeff approaching.

He grasped my arms lightly, though obviously detecting my mental turmoil. "What is it, Janet?"

"Nancy now believes I'm trying to drive her insane. She thinks I want her money."

His arm went around my waist. "I have some news which I hope will take your mind off Nancy."

"I pray it's good news. Certainly I could use some."

"At least it's news," he offered. "And that's something. You were right in identifying that hulk as the *Celtic*."

I sighed audibly, for his words did nothing to ease my anguish. "Well, at least we know. Perhaps it's as well. I doubt I could stay here much longer."

"I haven't finished," he said. "Five years ago the *Celtic* was sold—to Mr. Cyrus Plant of New York."

"That name has a familiar sound."

"You undoubtedly heard it from your father or your uncle. Mr. Plant had the ship rechristened after his wife—whose name was Cecelia."

"That's wonderful news!" I exclaimed, my spirits already lifting. "It means we're on to something. It means Uncle Lew was right."

"It does indeed," he agreed. "I feel as good about it as you. For a while, it looked as if we were riding a dead horse. The way I figure it, the newer paint, carrying the name, must have eroded away and allowed the underpaint to come through so you saw the original name."

"Which means I must stay here a while longer. For as long as it will take to clear Papa's name. Thank you for going to all the trouble of finding this out."

"Had to, for your sake."

"Oh," I said, suddenly remembering. "We had some visitors today. A Mr. Michael Yates, his daughter Daphne and his secretary Roy Lacey came to visit. They stopped only long enough to inform Nancy and me that they wanted to buy the entire bluff, tear down the house and build a very large and fancy resort hotel."

"That's interesting. Quite a boon for the villagers."

"I'm aware of that," I said coldly. "But I'm not interested."

90

Jeff said kindly, "I understand your bitterness, but don't let it sway your thinking. It's up to us to prove them wrong. We've already made a start by locating and identifyng the *Cecelia*. You can take pride in that. You must also, from now on, exercise great caution, for I'm convinced there are others aware of its location."

"Do you suppose the strangers who wish to buy the house are in some way mixed up in this?" I asked.

"I wonder," Jeff said. "I believe those bobbing lights and the voice calling your name were meant to frighten you away from here. Obviously that ruse has failed. It could well be these people have been sent here to purchase the house from you. The offer would be so attractive you could ill afford to refuse it. If it is, they or whoever is behind them will probably bear looking into."

"But why should they want the house?"

"I doubt they do," Jeff said. "I rather think their idea is still to get you away from these parts. With the house no longer in your possession, you'd have small reason to remain here. What did you say their names were?"

"The older gentleman's name is Mr. Michael Yates. His daughter Daphne is beautiful. Mr. Yates's secretary accompanied them. His name is Mr. Roy Lacey."

"The name Yates sounds familiar, but I can't place it. I'll make it a point to though."

"I'm anxious to make another dive to the yacht to see if I can uncover anything more," I said.

"We'll do it together. I don't want you out there alone," Jeff said. "Just now, I have to attend to my lobsters."

I was disappointed, for the sun was still high and I wanted to go out to the sunken hulk immediately. But I bade Jeff a cheery farewell and stood there, watching him until he was out of sight. I knew it could well be dangerous for me to go alone, but I was restless, impatient. I might discover some kind of proof of Papa's innocence in regard to the fate of the vessel.

My mind made up, I moved quickly to the boathouse where I changed to my bathing suit. I made sure there were sufficient rocks in the dory and then I rowed out until I located the red lobster trap below the surface of the water, marking the location of the wreck. I threw out the

91

sea anchor, shipped the oars and stood up with a heavy rock in each hand. I launched myself in as powerful a dive as I could muster from the dory. The rocks increased my impetus and I went down fast. In seconds, I was at the hulk. With only a minute left, I maneuvered about the large hole in the hull of the ship and I was able to make out objects still entrapped in the portion where the explosion had taken place.

I had to go up for air then. I rested, armed myself with more stones, dove and, even on the way down, it came to me that one of those objects I saw was a maple chair that should have been familiar to me. Papa never sailed without it because he stoutly maintained it was the only comfortable chair he'd ever sat on.

That meant the yawning aperture led directly into Papa's cabin. I was suddenly stricken with fresh horror at what I'd see if I managed to work my way into the wreck.

I grasped the edge of the hole, half lifted, half swam myself into the ship proper. It was very dark. I made my way more by sense of feel. My hands were touching a hard, smooth metal object. I used both hands and decided what I felt was a ship's safe.

I had to go up for air, but on my next dive I knew exactly where I was going. I wedged my way inside once more, this time feeling for the handle of the safe. I found it, turned the handle and, to my surprise, the door opened. I felt inside for a familiar object. The large, leather-bound log which my father always kept in the safe. My searching fingers closed around it.

I clung to the heavy book, fought my way to the surface and dropped the book into the dory. I clung to the side of it for several minutes to clear my head and reduce the dizziness from lack of air. I was trembling from my exertions and it was all I could do to hold onto the side, but I finally managed to pull myself aboard. I lay on the bottom of the boat awhile longer, until my heart ceased its mad pounding and my breath no longer came in gasps. The log beneath me cut into my thigh, but it was a welcome pain. I could scarcely wait to examine it.

Finally, my strength renewed, I moved up onto the seat. I let the book stay where it was, not daring to open the pages, for I was as wet as the book, which was swollen out of proportion with some of the leather binding already separated. However, the sheer weight of the covers and the book itself had been enough to preserve at least some of the pages. I was beside myself with excitement. Here, written by my father, could be the answer to this puzzle which had haunted me for so long.

I rowed back, my exultation such that I wasn't even feeling tired from my exertions. I reached the boathouse and, while dressing, I decided it would be wise not to let Nancy know I'd discovered the log. This was a secret I meant to share temporarily with no one but Jeff.

Therefore, when I reached the house, I opened the front door softly and listened for sounds of Nancy, but heard nothing. I closed the door softly, tiptoeing to the bottom of the stairs and started up them.

"Janet!" Nancy's voice was, all at once, sharp, angry and triumphant at having witnessed me attempting to outwit her. She'd been in the parlor, probably even watching for me. "What's that you're carrying?"

"Just a book," I said.

"And you have to sneak in with just a book in your hand? One that's dripping water? If it fell in the sea, why didn't you let it drift away?"

I decided on a little firmness myself. I was tired of her verbal abuse and though I was going to be deceitful, I felt it would be in a good cause. "I shouldn't have to sneak into my own house," I said quietly. "I did so only because I'm tired of quarreling with you."

With that I continued on to my room, though conscious of her eyes following me as I went up the stairs. She no doubt heard me continue on to the next floor, for I was on my way to the lookout room. I knew she wouldn't follow me up here, for she disliked the room. I sat down at my uncle's desk, place the log before me and managed to lift the cover enough to see my father's handwriting. He'd inscribed his name and the date when the log was first used.

I tried to open some of the pages, but the book would have to dry or I might destroy everything. Much of the ink had faded or run, but I could see words on some of the pages. I decided to risk opening it at about the middle. If the binding broke, that would be no hazard to the pages. So, with my breath held and a prayer on my lips, I carefully slid my fingers between the pages. The paper crumpled somewhat, but it didn't tear or stick.

I opened the book flat now and bent over the pages. The familiar writing tore at my heart, but I managed to suppress the threatened tears and then found myself reading a brief but unexpected chronicle of events aboard the yacht just before the wireless message was sent.

June 23, 1893. Sailing north by northwest, sea calm, speed normal. This is a fine ship. Passengers are comfortable and prepared to disembark tomorrow. It has been an uneventful voyage for which I am most grateful. I am carrying many of the nation's most eminent people and I feel the responsibility for providing them with a safe passage.

Have just discovered two stowaways in the forward hold. They claim they only wish to return to the United States after some unprofitable adventures in Europe. Mr. Cyrus Plant, the owner of this yacht, advises they should be put to work. There won't be much for them to do as we are rapidly nearing port. I shall turn them over to authorities to be held for immigration officers in case they are lying and are aliens. Talked with both and I must confess they seem sly and shady. I do not trust them.

That was all, but it created in me the greatest of hope that I was at last beginning to get at the truth.

It was possible other pages in the book would be as profitable, but I dared not open them until they had dried. I did manage to ascertain the entry I'd read was the last one in the book. The following pages were blank. Therefore, I thought, it made little difference if the pages behind it were damaged. I made a wad of about eight pages, lifted them free and then carefully removed the sodden sheets from the book itself. The important page was intact. I placed it on a hard chair which I moved into the rays of sunlight. The book itself would never dry well unless it had air so I carried it up to the widow's walk and laid it in the warm afternoon sun, holding it down with a pair of heavy bookends taken from my uncle's desk.

Excitement reminded me that I was hungry, but as I prepared to leave the room, I hesitated at allowing that important page to be so openly displayed. I cleared one drawer in the roll top, placed the pages directly on the bottom of the drawer and then lightly covered them with some of Uncle Lew's papers. Later, I could place them in the sunlight once again.

I dreaded going downstairs for a further confrontation, but the sea air, coupled with my exertions in diving, had sharpened my hunger. I was about to look in the ice box for something to warm when my nostrils were assailed by the tangy fragrance of ham. I found a plate in the oven for me. I had to smile despite myself. While Nancy made no attempt to hide her dislike for me, she wasn't going to see me go hungry, and though I'd missed my midday meal, she'd kept it warm for me. It assured me that, somewhere in her mind, she had an occasional kind thought about me.

I sat down and ate slowly, all the while wondering about what could have happened on the yacht that night. Two stowaways who'd been clever enough to avoid detection until the final night at sea. Stowing away in a private yacht was unusual. Customarily, only the large liners were used because there were a hundred more places in which to hide.

I wondered who the two were. It was obvious that if any of the passengers or crew had managed to get ashore in the lifeboat, that person would surely have come forward. If, however, the stowaways made use of the boat, they were unlikely to tell anyone what had happened. Especially, I thought, if they had made it happen.

There were so many channels to investigate, and so many theories had abounded in my mind, but I now had a fresh outlook because those stowaways had a meaning and this was the first time their presence was known.

I hoped Jeff would pay me a visit tonight. I was impatient to tell him about my discovery and to listen to any ideas he might have in regard to the stowaways.

I finished eating and realized I'd taken quite some time about it. I was doing the dishes when I heard the front door close. I stood listening for a few moments, but I heard no voices, no sound of anyone coming in. I hung up the dish towel, then went to the parlor. Nancy wasn't there. Puzzled, I went to the front door, opened it and saw her walking quickly in the direction of the village. She had one of her large, fringed shawls draped over her shoulders and gathered about her. I wondered what message she was carrying to Abner this time.

I decided to take advantage of the fact that she was out of the house. She's surely be gone for forty or fifty minutes. Time enough to bring down the log book and place it in the barely warm oven. That would help. I could also dry the pages I'd removed from the book.

I hurried to the third floor, continuing on up the ladder to the widow's walk. The two bookends were there, but the log was gone! It had been taken only moments before because the deck still bore the marks from the dampness of the large book. I thought of those precious pages I'd placed in the desk drawer. Could they have been taken also?

Panic-stricken at the thought, I turned quickly. My heel came down on something that threw me off balance and I reached out, gripping the rail for support. Perhaps, if I hadn't been so shaken by the absence of the log book, I'd have been more cautious, for it was perilous up here. The rail was low and I could easily have gone over, but, fortunately, I was in excellent trim and my grip was strong. I quickly regained my balance and glanced down to see what I'd stepped on. It looked like a pebble. Curious, I picked it up, wondering how the wind could have carried it to such a height.

When I examined it more carefully, I discovered it was a piece of metal, badly corroded. I turned it over and observed the underside revealed a small slot through which thread or string could pass. Then I knew! It was a button which I recognized as the type decorating a uniform. A captain's uniform! Papa's uniform!

My fingers closed around it, more in wonderment than in fear. Could it somehow have got caught in the book? It seemed unlikely. Had it been placed here to frighten me? Was I supposed to believe Papa came out of the sea to retrieve the log book? Would Nancy have resorted to such chicanery?

Were those two precious pages I'd placed in the drawer still there? I dropped the button into my dress pocket and descended the ladder carefully. Scarcely daring to breathe, I opened the drawer slowly, sighing in relief when I saw the pages there, intact. I carried them downstairs and placed them in a baking pan which I thrust into the oven, taking the precaution of leaving the door wide open.

I stood near a window which fronted the house so I'd be able to see Nancy returning. It had to be Nancy who'd taken the log. She'd concealed it beneath that large shawl. She'd be bringing it to no one but Abner who had shown far too much interest in what was going on here.

She'd observed me returning to the house with the log. She had a good opportunity of seeing it when she called to me as I stealthily ascended the stairs. She'd even commented on the wet book. No doubt she'd guessed what it was, for log books looked much alike. She'd heard me continue on up to the third floor. When I went down to the kitchen, she'd slipped up there and discovered the book. Could it be that someone in the village—Abner—knew the wreck of the *Cecelia* lay out there? Had he enlisted the help of Nancy to observe my comings and goings? Would she have gone to such an extreme to attempt to frighten me? I knew she resented the fact that Uncle Lew had left me the house. Perhaps because of that she'd been a willing ally, while all the time pretending I was trying to drive her out of the house. Yet I had no proof and without it I'd not condemn her.

Besides, I wanted no more troublesome scenes. I'd make no mention of the book to her until I'd discussed its loss with Jeff.

I removed the pan containing the precious papers from the stove and put the pan away. The pages were almost dry. I hastened upstairs to conceal them, this time in my room. I moved swiftly to a window where I observed Nancy approaching the house, more slowly this time, for she carried a large sack of groceries, which were no doubt the gift of Abner as a reward for her services. At the same time that thought occurred to me, I believed I heard the sound of a door closing in the house. I was puzzled by it and more than a little startled, for it wasn't Nancy. She was still in my line of vision. Then I dismissed the thought as the result of nerves brought on by the loss of the log book.

SEVEN

I didn't go down for supper, nor did Nancy summon me. I wasn't hungry and I knew conversation between us would be difficult. I remained in my room, sorely disappointed that Jeff had not put in an appearance. I had so much to tell him. I had learned a great deal since I'd last seen him.

I moved languidly to the window, straining my eyes for a hopeful glimpse of his sturdy form, but neither he nor his boat were in sight. I watched the sun begin to sink beneath the horizon. Suddenly it was blotted out as a wall of fog made its appearance and I heard the first wail of the fog horn. A strange and unwelcome feeling began to creep over me, in much the same way as the fog bank making its stealthy way toward land to encompass and enclose everything.

I settled myself in a chair. I don't know how long I sat there, alone with my thoughts, but I remember seeing the fog, even in darkness, drift past my window. I hoped Jeff was outside, keeping a sharp eye on the house. I wondered if he would choose the protection of the front veranda. At least it would offer him a slight shelter from the dampness of the fog. The thought of him being there lifted my spirits and I decided to go down.

I arose, lit a lamp when a sharp scream cut the silence. My brain reeled in sudden panic. It was Nancy's voice, filled with terror and I believed it came from downstairs. I left my room and moved swiftly to the staircase. She was slowly backing away from the front door, which was opened wide.

"Nancy," I called out. "Nancy, what is it?"

Without turning, she cried out, "Come down, Janet. Please come down."

I hastened down the stairs, set my lamp on a table, closed the front door and turned to her. Her breath was coming in gasps and she seemed frozen in fear. She was pressed hard against the wall, probably using it as a support, for she was trembling visibly.

"What is it?" I asked, keeping my voice calm in an effort to ease her terror.

"Eli . . . your papa!" Her arm raised and she pointed a finger at the closed door. "He's out there. I saw him!"

"Nonsense," I said sternly. "Papa's dead. He went down with his ship. You know it as well as I."

She nodded. "His ghost . . . his ghost. He was wearing his uniform. It was wet, like he came out of the water. He had no face."

I moved up to her, my hands resting on her shoulders, but she pushed me back, terror seemingly having robbed her of all reason.

"You wouldn't deliberately frighten me, would you, Janet? Would you?" She was like a child, pleading for reassurance.

"I've never tried to frighten you," I said.

"Abner said you did." Her words were almost a babble. "Abner said you wanted me out of here. He said . . ." Her voice trailed off.

"He said I wanted to kill you," I finished. "That I probably pushed Uncle Lew off the cliff."

"Yes," she whimpered. "Yes, he said all that. But you wouldn't kill me, would you?"

"No, Auntie, I wouldn't." For the first time since she'd told me not to address her so, I'd used the affectionate appellation. "Believe me, Auntie. Trust me, I beg of you."

"The book you had this afternoon," she said. "It was a log book, wasn't it?"

"Yes," I replied without the slightest hesitation. I had to tell her. I was tired of secrets and deceit. "Why did you take it to Abner?"

"I didn't," she said, and I knew she spoke the truth. I remembered then that, while watching her approach the house, I thought I'd heard a door close.

100

"You went to see Abner," I said.

She nodded. "I told him you had a log book. I told him you were trying to sneak upstairs without me seeing you. I said the book was wet. That it must have fallen in the sea."

"But you didn't take it to him?" I asked, more puzzled than ever.

"Honest, Janet," she said. "Please believe me."

"I do, Aunt Nancy," I replied. My arms enclosed her and this time she didn't draw away. I was filled with pity for this woman and I didn't know how to reassure her. "I'm going outside and see if there's anyone moving about."

"Don't open the door," she begged. "I heard the haunt walking back and forth across the veranda. I thought it was Jeff, but I should have known better."

"It could have been Jeff," I said, not quite believing it. "I know he's outside somewhere guarding this house. He's fearful someone wants to do away with me."

"Jeff isn't out there," she said. "That . . . that spook is out there."

"Please let me open the door and look," I asked, holding her at arm's length.

"I'll stay right with you," she insisted. "Right by your side."

"Very well." I turned to the table and picked up the lamp. "Maybe you'd like to take a lamp too."

"I don't think I could hold one."

"Stay close beside me then." I spoke with quiet assurance.

I opened the door and we stepped outside. I held the lamp up.

"There's no one out here," I said.

"What's that?" Nancy said. She pointed a finger downward. I could see something glisten and lowered the lamp. I reached down and picked it up, holding it close to the lamp, though I knew full well what it was. Seaweed! Nancy gave a terrified cry and ran inside.

I threw the alga over the porch rail and followed her, closing the door behind me.

"Now do you believe me?" she wailed.

"I believe someone's trying to frighten both of us." I spoke with a calmness I was far from feeling.

"It could be your young man," she said. Then, more firmly. "It could be. He was at the village inn this afternoon with that Daphne girl that came here. He was certainly attentive to her."

"Are you sure?" I asked, aghast at such news. Jeff had told me he had his lobster traps to attend to.

She nodded. "Abner told me about it. I told Abner it wasn't so, that Jeff was quite smitten with you."

I couldn't help but smile. "I thought he was too, Auntie. Or do you mind my calling you Auntie?"

"No, child," she said. "I've been mighty mean to you. And I'm scared now. Somehow I feel I'm not long for this world. I think that haunt came to take me."

"Don't talk that way, Auntie," I said. "You're overwrought. You've let Abner convince you that I'm up to something. Perhaps even that Jeff is up to something. I refuse to believe that. I'm positive he's out there now somewhere, guarding our safety."

"Get him," Nancy pleaded. "Get him inside. Ask him to stay with us. We need a man here. I'm scared clear through."

"All right," I agreed. "I'll go outside and call him. He'll be patrolling somewhere around. I suggest you go to your room and lock yourself in."

"I'm scared to go up there," she said.

"I'll go with you and check your room to make certain there's no one about." I was thinking of the sound of the closing door I'd heard this afternoon and wondered if someone really was hidden in the house. I wondered what it was Nancy had seen. Or who it was. I couldn't believe it had been all in her mind. She was too frightened to be pretending.

Upstairs, I looked under her bed, moved the clothes in her closet to make certain no one was concealed behind them.

"There's no one in this room," I told her. "I suggest you move a piece of furniture against your door. Don't open it for anybody."

"I'll have to recognize your voice before I even open it

for you," she said. "I'm scared clear through, child. I believe everything you said now. I just want you to know it."

"Thank you, Auntie," I replied. Impulsively, I kissed her cheek. "I'll be back shortly. It may take a while to locate Jeff because I have to move cautiously in the fog."

"I'll sit here and wait for you after I push this chest against the door."

She was already moving the cumbersome piece as I picked up the lamp. I went down to the kitchen, knowing there was a lantern there and it would be much easier to handle, especially in the fog, for I had to beware of moving too far from the house. I could easily become lost in the fog and find myself at the edge of the cliff. I shuddered at the thought.

I started out, calling Jeff's name. I moved slowly, starting to circle the house, trying not to get too far from it. It loomed like a black monster in the clammy gray curtain. Then I heard a sound and looked about me. I felt prickles of fear edge along my spine, for I could see no one. The squeaking of the rusty handle of the lantern grated on my nerves as I continued my search. I wondered why Jeff had forsaken me. If he really believed I was in danger, why did he leave me at the mercy of whoever sought to do me harm?

Then I heard it, ever so softly now, the hollow, melancholy sound of someone calling my name. At first, I couldn't locate the direction from which it came. Certainly, even if there were bobbing lights at sea, I'd not see them on such a night. Suddenly I realized the voice seemed to be coming from the house. Yet that seemed impossible. I could still see its dark outline and I stopped to listen. Slowly my eyes raised to the widow's walk. There was a light up there! A strong one which managed to pierce the fog. While I stared, into its gleam came a figure. It wore the uniform of a ship's captain, even to the hat. At this distance it was impossible to make out the features. Then, as if it was aware of the thought that passed through my mind, I saw the hat removed and I stared at nothing. There was no face, yet I could still see the form, its arms now extended in an entreating gesture.

103

Then the light faded and so did the sound of my name. I wondered how long I'd stood there, for I seemed frozen to the spot. I had no idea of how many times my name had been called. I wondered if my aunt had heard it. If so, I hoped she'd not left the sanctuary of her room.

I was trembling now and as filled with fear as she when I left her, but I had to return to the house. I couldn't leave that poor woman there alone. Even at this moment, I could feel a great measure of gratification that we were closer than we'd ever been. I knew now she was a lonely, frightened person, drawn to Abner only because of that. I believed he had duped her, thought I didn't know if she was yet aware of it.

I had just reached the steps when I heard a horrible scream, quickly cut off. I knew it was my aunt and though it seemed to be outside, I ran into the house and up the steps, the light from the lantern making crazy patterns on the wall.

I reached her room and groaned when I saw the door opened wide. She was nowhere in sight. Somehow she must have been lured from it. Or had she been listening to me call Jeff and when she heard my name called, thought it might be he answering my summons.

There was no sign of her. Could she have gone up to the lookout room or the widow's walk? I prayed not and, forcing myself every step of the way, I went up there to find it empty. I lit two lamps to reassure myself there was no one up here. I didn't know if I'd be signing my doom if I ventured up the ladder to the widow's walk, but I had to find Nancy. Perhaps she'd been taken from her room and brought here as a means of luring me here also.

I stepped out the door and moved to the ladder. My foot touched something soft, and I moaned aloud in despair. Even before I moved the lantern to reveal what blocked my path, I knew what I'd find. Nor was I wrong. The body of my aunt lay in a grotesque heap. She'd either fallen or been thrown from the widow's walk to the rooftop below. From the grotesque position of her head, I knew her neck had been broken. Nevertheless I felt for a pulse. There was none. There was nothing I could do for Nancy. I dared not even lift her.

The horror of the past minutes now flooded through me and, half hysterical, I got up, retraced my steps to my room and got a shawl. Still carrying the lantern, I went downstairs and out the front door, not even bothering to close it behind me. I didn't think the house was in danger; only the occupants . . . one now. I was on my way to the village, not even certain I'd be allowed to reach it. Not knowing if the fog would close in about me so intensely I'd be lured miles out of my way. But I couldn't remain alone in that house.

I don't know how long I walked, but finally I caught a glimpse of a light and headed for it. Ironically, it was the inn, where Nancy had told me she'd seen Jeff with Daphne. I wondered if he'd still be there and breathed a prayer he would. For some reason, it seemed more important I reach him than the constable. I suppose I wanted his comforting presence.

And when I walked through the door, his was the first face I saw. The second was Daphne. They were seated, facing each other, and they seemed to be engaged in an earnest conversation until Jeff, as if suddenly aware of my presence, turned and our eyes met. I suppose I looked a little ridiculous holding onto the lantern, but the way he jumped up and came to me, I knew my face must still reveal the horror of what I'd gone through.

He took the lantern from me and brought me outside. "What's happened?"

"Aunt Nancy is dead," I said, my voice dull. "She either fell or was pushed off the widow's walk."

"Wait here." He returned seconds later. "Come along. I've told the proprietor to send word to the constable. We'll get right back to the house."

On the way, I told him all that happened. My discovery of the log that afternoon, followed by its disappearance and how I'd thought my aunt had taken it to Abner, though she'd denied it tonight and I believed her.

"Tonight my aunt said she saw the ghost of my father on the veranda," I said. "I went out there to find seaweed on the veranda. I found a button this afternoon on the widow's walk. It looked as if it had come from Papa's uniform. It was badly corroded."

105

I knew the things I spoke of were not given in chronological order, but my mind was still filled with confusion and terror and I believe I was in partial shock.

"Forgive me, my darling, for not having been here to prevent what happened," Jeff said.

"Why did you let me down?" I asked in bewilderment. "Why?"

"I didn't mean to." His arm, around my waist, tightened. "I'm horrified by what you've told me. I feel myself responsible for your aunt's death."

"Perhaps it would have happened anyway," I said. "Maybe I was the one meant to be killed. I don't know. I think, though, that someone has access to the house."

"Some must have," Jeff agreed. "Someone who is bent on driving you from the house."

"Or killing me," I amended.

"God forbid," he said.

It seemed an endless time until we reached the house. The door was open, just as I left it. I accompanied Jeff upstairs as far as the lookout room where the lamps still burned.

"You'd better stay inside," he said, urging me to my uncle's chair.

I gave him no argumeent, for I didn't think my limbs would hold me up much longer. He went outside and I saw him hold the lamp above the form of what I knew was the earthly remains of my aunt. He momentarily disappeared from view as he bent over her.

When he stood up, he had her in his arms. "Lead me to her room," he said.

I left the lamps burning and took the lantern. We went down the flight of stairs, turned and entered Nancy's room. I noticed five lamps burning in her room. She truly had been terrified, yet she had been induced to open the door.

I told Jeff of my theory in regard to her death.

"It could be either," he said. "It's up to us to find out exactly what happened. And we will."

He set her on the bed tenderly and closed the eyes that stared unseeingly at the ceiling. I covered her still body with a sheet and Jeff led me from the room.

"They'll be here soon from the village," he said. "No one can harm her further. Let's go downstairs. I want you to go over what you told me on the way back."

We went to the parlor and Jeff lit the fireplace. He urged it into a bright flame with the bellows and he drew a chair close to the one I occupied.

"Before you begin," he said, "I want to show you something that was clutched in your aunt's hand."

He took a small object from his pocket, but before he extended his hand, I told him what it was.

"It's a button from a captain's uniform," I said. "To further bear out the story my aunt told me of seeing my father's faceless ghost."

"Yes," he said. "Does it resemble the one you found on the widow's walk this afternoon?"

I glanced at it, though not deigning to touch it. "It's identical." I slipped my hand into my own pocket, placed its mate in Jeff's hand.

"I'll keep these for the time being," he said.

I regarded him curiously. "Why didn't you tell me about it upstairs? I mean, when you brought my aunt's body into my uncle's den . . . when you were carrying her body . . ."

"Janet," Jeff said, "are you suspicious of me? Don't you trust me? Do you think I want to drive you away from here—to kill you?"

"I don't know," I cried out. "I'm so frightened."

"I know you are," he said. "You've been very brave. Try to trust me. I love you. Whether you believe it or not, it's the truth."

Such was my state of mind that the words which should have sent a joyous feeling of ecstasy through me were almost without meaning.

"Darling Janet," he said and reached for my hands. I clenched them into fists and held them at my side, my glance defiant.

"Forgive me," he said, settling back. "If you don't wish to speak, I'll understand. However, I'll not leave you alone here until the constable comes. And I'll not leave even then until I know you'll not be alone here tonight."

I suppose those words were what decided me, for I

relented, held out my hands for him to take. "I'm sorry, Jeff. For a moment I was as suspicious of you as Nancy was of me, even tonight. But I thank God, during her last few moments on earth, we were reconciled. I need you, Jeff. All the way to the village I prayed you'd be there, even if you were with Daphne. Nancy told me about that. Abner told her."

"Abner figures quite prominently in all of this, doesn't he?" Jeff said, his voice suddenly cold. "For the moment though, we've got to forget him. You told me about the log book being stolen. And you mentioned the pages you'd salvaged which revealed information concerning the two stowaways."

"Yes, I still have those pages unless they've been pilfered from my room," I said.

"I'd like to see them," he said. "Now I'll go up with you."

We were in the reception hall when the sound of approaching vehicles interrupted us. Jeff said, "Say nothing about those pages. We'll discuss them later."

I opened the door to greet Silas Bixby who was the constable. Also present were Abner Pauley, Michael Yates, the speculator who wanted to buy the house, and his secretary Roy Lacey. Behind them, as if unsure of her welcome, was Daphne Yates. Why they came, I had no idea, but I was grateful. Besides the carriages, I also noticed a hearse parked a short distance from the house. I knew Jeff must have ordered it and I appreciated his thoughtfulness.

The gentlemen spoke words of sympathy, after which Jeff led Silas Lacey upstairs. I motioned Mr. Yates and Mr. Lacey into the parlor along with Daphne, telling them I'd go into the kitchen and put on a pot of coffee. Daphne insisted on remaining with me.

"I'm so sorry, Janet," she said, taking a seat at the table. "Such a horrible death."

"Yes," I said. "My aunt did nothing to deserve such a fate. Nor did my uncle."

"I heard about that," she said. "Two dreadful accidents occuring in a matter of days."

"I'm not so sure they were accidents," I said. I already had the coffee on the stove and I discovered an elderberry

108

pie in the refrigerator. I suppose Nancy had baked it for Abner, expecting him to make another visit. Well, he had, though the occasion was a tragic one. I placed the pie in the oven and set the table.

"Surely you won't stay here," Daphne said. "I could never remain in a house alone where there had been such a horrible accident."

I'd been on the point of asking her to come here as my guest, for I'd have welcomed her company, but I dismissed the thought. I'd manage. I heard the thump of the casket bumping the wall a few times as it was carried down the stairs. The men's voices, though subdued, carried to the kitchen. I asked Daphne if she'd summon them. I poured the coffee and cut the pie, giving each of them a generous serving. I had no appetite and when they entered the kitchen, I waited to see if they had what they wished, then excused myself and went to the parlor. I was grateful now to be alone. Jeff wisely remained with the group, granting me a few minutes of privacy. I sat in the parlor and though the fire burned brightly, I felt chilled to the bone. I wondered if I'd ever feel warm again. After a while, I heard Jeff bid the group farewell. I heard the vehicles drive off and the soft closing of the door.

A moment later, he entered. "I told the constable you'd talk with him tomorrow."

"Thanks, Jeff," I said. "I appreciate it."

"Do you feel capable of discussing anything connected with this awful business? Or do you wish to retire?"

"I want terribly to talk about it with you," I said. "I feel we must work very fast if we're going to discover the reason behind this. I'm sure my aunt was murdered, just as my uncle was."

"I'm of the same opinion," he said. "I also believe your life is in jeopardy. However, they may exercise more restraint now, for I expressed the idea to the constable that I questioned Nancy's death was accidental. I said it in front of Abner and the others who came."

"I can understand Abner's presence," I said. "But why the others?"

"They said they wished to offer you comfort."

I couldn't help but smile. "I almost asked Daphne to

stay until she stated she could never live in a house of tragedy. She urged me to come to the inn. Naturally I refused. I'm going to remain here. I believe someone has access to this house. Who it is, or how he gets in, I have no idea, but late this afternoon I thought I heard a door close in the house. At that very moment I was at my window, watching my aunt return from the village."

Jeff's mouth tightened. "They're trying to force you to believe your father's ghost is haunting this house. They fooled Nancy into believing it. They probably even lured her to the widow's walk."

"It has to be something like that," I said. "I was outside calling your name. Then that same mournful voice called my name, though this time it didn't drift across the water. I looked up at the widow's walk and saw a light there. Then the form of a man wearing a captain's uniform, even to the hat. When he removed it, there was no face. My aunt saw the same thing on the veranda. When we went out to look, there was wet seaweed just beyond the portal."

"Preposterous," Jeff said, his tone scornful.

"I know," I said. "But she believed it was the ghost of my father."

"All right, my darling," he said. "First of all, tell me about the log."

"I found the safe. It was just inside that terrible hole blown into the hull of the ship. I grasped the handle, turned it and pulled. . . ."

"Then the safe wasn't locked."

"No," I said, frowning. "But my father never left it unlocked. Surely the safe must have contained some valuables?"

"Some?" he said, with a touch of derision. "Remember, Janet, the yacht carried wives of ten of the wealthiest men in the United States. They'd just returned from attending a gala—the crowning of royalty. No matter that it was a small, practically unheard-of country—an invitation to it was one of the social plums of the year. Those women would certainly have brought all the jewelry they possessed. Offhand, I should say it must have been worth several million dollars."

110

"And such valuables would be kept in the ship's safe," I reasoned.

"Yes," he said.

"Then why wasn't the safe locked?" I drew in a sharp breath, as a sudden thought came to me. "Jeff! Someone forced my father to open the safe!"

"Will you show me the pages from the log?" he asked.

"Of course." I arose and picked up a lamp, which he took from my hand. Upstairs he remained outside my door while I got the pages which I'd placed beneath the bed. Downstairs again, he examined them.

"The yacht was only a matter of an hour's run from the village," he said, "when your father wrote that entry about the stowaways. That meant if the ship caught fire—and it certainly wasn't burning when he made his entry—the glow would have been seen. Also, I don't think any fire could have consumed that yacht so quickly that it couldn't have been beached from that distance at sea."

"It was blown up," I said. "That's what it looks like from the hole in its side."

Jeff looked doubtful. "An explosion might have been heard. It could have happened while the ship was far enough out so it wouldn't be heard on land, and the ship floated long enough to reach this spot. By then it must have shipped so much water that it rolled over and sank."

I had some misgivings about the theory. "Jeff, anyone who could swim could have made it to shore. Or they could have sent up a rocket, or screamed . . . or something. How could the ship have just gone down without anyone aboard not having heard the explosion or not be aware something was wrong?"

"The logical explanation is that everyone on board was dead. Either the explosion had killed them . . . or the stowaways."

"Can the jewels still be aboard?" I asked.

"It's possible, because we really don't know what happened the night of the sinking. But with the safe door unlocked I hardly think so."

"And do you believe what's happened here has something to do with that act of piracy and murder?"

"I believe it has everything to do with it."

111

"Then Uncle Lew was murdered because he discovered something."

"Yes, and if we can prove even some of this, that wireless message from the yacht can surely be made out to have been false. Therefore the accusation made against your father is completely mendacious."

"We must learn who those stowaways were, for obviously they used the lifeboat to escape to safety," I said earnestly. "They will provide us with the answer. Only they can clear Papa's name, for they must have been responsible for the deaths of everyone on board the yacht. Now there are the added murders of my aunt and uncle."

"We have no proof your aunt and uncle were murdered," Jeff said remindfully. "That's what we must get. And we'll start working on it tomorrow. Just now you need rest. With your permission, I'll remain outside your room tonight. If you have a sleeping draught, I'd advise you to take it."

"I have a powder," I said.

"I'm going to check your room first, just to make certain all is well," he said, picking up a lamp.

It was comforting to be looked after, but his words reminded me of those I'd said to my aunt this same night. Yet I was glad I'd searched her room, for at least I knew there'd been no one concealed there when she placed the chest in front of her door.

After he'd made a thorough search of the room, he said, "Just before you get into bed, please open your door a few inches. In that way, I'll hear any untoward sound."

I handed him a comforter with which he could wrap himself up. He had moved an easy chair from my room to the hall and placed it beside a small table on which set a lamp. The precious pages of the log rested on the table.

"I'll study the remaining words on these pages and see if I can learn anything more," Jeff said, his eyes on the log.

112

EIGHT

I awoke to daylight, and a remembrance of the events of the night. I arose, reluctant to begin my day. My tasks would not be pleasant, but they had to be faced.

On the hall table there was a note from Jeff, stating he'd made a thorough search of the house, finding no evidence of anyone being present, or of anyone having forced an entrance. Therefore, I reasoned, someone had to have a key, because I would not believe it was Papa's ghost which had caused my aunt's tragic death.

I dressed quickly, choosing a dark blue tailor-made. I'd stop by the dressmaker's when I was in the village in the hope that she might have a black ready-made which would fit me. I'd ruined mine in the fall near the cliff. I breakfasted lightly and would not have bothered except that I hadn't eaten since the previous afternoon.

I was just about to go upstairs to Nancy's room to gather some garments to bring to the undertaker's when the knocker on the front door reverberated through the house. Without the slightest fear, I opened it. Jeff gathered me in his arms and for a long moment neither of us spoke.

"I left as soon as the fog lifted," he said, releasing me. "I just stopped by to see what I could do for you."

"Not a thing," I said. "I have several chores to attend to in the village. But thanks anyway. There is one thing I'd like to ask you though. What did you do with those precious pages of the log?"

"I mailed them this morning to a friend who will see that they're placed in the proper hands, once we learn a little more about this," Jeff said.

"Don't you think the constable should see them?" I asked.

"Not yet," Jeff said. "We'll keep it our secret."

"Whatever you say," I agreed. "But I must stop in and tell him what happened."

"Will you tell him about the ghost?" Jeff asked somberly.

"I don't know," I said, frowning thoughtfully. "How can I? He'll think I'm losing my mind."

"If Abner hears the story, he might accuse you of making up the tale," Jeff said.

The sudden realization of what Jeff meant came to me. "You're right. Abner told Aunt Nancy I could well have murdered Uncle Lew."

Jeff nodded. "I think you'd better say nothing."

"But you mentioned to the constable you thought it might not be an accident," I said remindfully. "And I said the same thing to Daphne."

"Did you give her any reason for your opinion?"

"No."

"In that case, why not just tell the constable you don't know how it happened," Jeff suggested. "It won't really be a lie."

"You're right, Jeff . . . as usual," I said with a sigh. "We must be very cautious. However, I don't like protecting a murderer."

"Nor I," he agreed. "But we have no choice until we obtain more proof. I'll see the constable sometime today and change my story. Just now I must attend to my lobsters. But I'll be here tonight. I'll not let you down again."

His kiss was fleeting, but the day was not one for lovemaking. I bade him farewell and went back upstairs. There, I packed my aunt's clothes, arranged a shawl on my shoulders and started out for the village.

My visit with the undertaker, who also ran the furniture store, was brief. He was properly sympathetic. I asked the funeral be held the following morning. He agreed and I took my leave, heading for the constable's office.

Mr. Bixby was very kind. I had fashioned a story in my

mind while I walked to the village and I recited it quietly, hoping he'd not question me. I told him that my aunt had gone to her room, while I stepped out on the veranda for a bit of exercise. I heard her scream and ran inside. When I found her room empty, I searched the house, finally finding her prostrate, lifeless body at the foot of the ladder leading to the widow's walk.

He asked me if I'd seen any evidence of foul play. I replied I had not, careful not to make any mention of the corroded metal button Jeff had found clasped in her hand. Had it been placed there deliberately to frighten me further? I wondered. If so, it had served its purpose.

Mr. Bixby thanked me for stopping by and I thanked him for not having pressed me with questions last night. He said he believed my aunt had gone up there for some unknown reason and had lost her footing while descending the ladder. I nodded agreement, not trusting myself to speak further.

I took my leave and went to the dressmaker's. I didn't know if she would speak to me, but, much to my surprise, her manner was courteous, even if not friendly. I was unable to make the purchase of a dress suitable for mourning, so I'd have to wear my navy blue tailor-made. However, I did have my black hat with veil.

I left the dressmaker's prepared to return to my home when Mr. Lacey blocked my path.

"Good morning, Miss Vance," he said. "Though it couldn't be, since I know your business here today is of a sad nature." He motioned with his hat in the direction of the undertaker.

"It is, but I've completed my business and am now returning to my home."

"Pray allow me to invite you to lunch. As you know, the inn serves excellent food."

I wasn't at all interested in food, but I was interested in Mr. Lacey, as to why he'd sought me out. "Thank you, sir. I accept."

The food was excellent and I must admit I enjoyed it. I also felt the time spent was worthwhile, in view of the ensuing conversation.

"I'm grateful for your charming company," Mr. Lacey said. "Also, I felt I've kept you out of that dreary house for a while."

"I don't consider it dreary," I replied. "I'm quite comfortable there."

"But in view of what happened, you're not remaining." He looked quite shocked.

"I am, indeed." I spoke over the rim of my cup. "There's been a great deal of tragedy in my life, but the house is not to blame."

"You mean you'd live alone there?"

"I do. Why should you look so downcast?"

"For a purely selfish reason," he said. "I was hopeful that if you intended to sell it—and I'd like to think I could convince you—you'd let me tell Mrs. Yates it was I who convinced you to do so."

"Why should I do such a thing?"

"It would be quite a pat on the back for me."

I touched my napkin to my lips. "Should I decide to sell, you will be the first person I shall inform."

"My eternal gratitude," he said. "And now, I beg of you, allow me to drive you back."

I did, for I was beginning to weary. I wasn't certain if it was because of the various places I'd been, or if Mr. Lacey was responsible. Not a very kind thought after the delicious repast I'd had at his expense, but I found him quite a bore.

I was busy for the remainder of the day with household duties. I searched Nancy's room, hopeful for some clue which might lead to her murderer. I went up on the widow's walk, but found nothing there. No one from the village paid a sympathy call. I'd hoped Daphne might come, but apparently the house frightened her. I couldn't blame her, as with the coming of night I felt a growing uneasiness.

I ate a light supper, did the dishes and moved out to the reception hall. With the oncoming of darkness, I lit three lamps there and in the parlor, I lit six. I had cleaned the fireplace, built a fire in it and now I lit it, hoping its crackling flames would lighten my spirits.

I longed for Jeff to come and wondered why he hadn't.

Was tonight going to be a repetition of last night? If so, I feared for my sanity. I thought of going to the village and taking a room at the inn, but I forced the thought from my mind. Murder had been done here and an attempt at murder had been made on my person. I had to remain and see this through. I had to learn who was behind it.

I now had every lamp in the house glowing brightly, but the slightest creak, or rustle of a branch brushing against the house made me start up in terror. I had never in my life felt so alone and so vulnerable. I finally found sufficient courage to step onto the porch and call Jeff's name. There was no reply. I hastily returned to the house and locked the door. There was nothing left for me to do now but retire. The very thought of it terrified me, yet I extinguished all the lamps save the one I'd carry with me.

I took elaborate preparations with my toilet and I knew why. I feared sleep. Yet I must have it. Tomorrow, the funeral would take place and I'd need all the rest I could get.

Finally, I turned down the lamp and, as was my wont, opened a window. Ten minutes later, I heard the doleful voice calling my name over and over again.

"Jannnnn . . . ettttt." Calling so slowly it seemed to drift in on the wind.

I knew if I looked out I'd see the strange red lights bobbing around while the voice sang its ghostly song. Tonight it seemed to go on and on. When I could bear it no longer, I got out of bed, put on slippers and wrapper, turned up the lamp as I picked it up and hastened downstairs. I ran to open the front door and dashed out into the night, still holding the lamp.

I didn't know where I was going, only that I could no longer remain here or I'd go mad. I felt danger and terror crowding in all around me. I needed help. I needed Jeff and, once again, he wasn't here.

Then someone dashed from the cover of a row of shrubs. I screamed and dropped the lamp as I tried to get away, but strong arms encircled me. A voice spoke and all the terror seemed to drain out of me. I was in Jeff's arms.

I twisted about and when I raised my face, he kissed me and held me close.

117

"It was the voice, wasn't it?" he asked gently.

"The voice and the lights," I sobbed.

"I know. I heard your name called and I saw the red lights."

"I didn't even know you were here. I called to you earlier in the evening."

"I . . . must have been down at the bluff. You're shivering. We'd better go inside."

I nodded, happily now. I wasn't afraid any more. I no longer had any doubts about Jeff and that was most important of all. When the door closed on us, I felt even safer. I remained by his side while he lit the lamps in the hall and those in the parlor. He guided me over to the settee and placed an arm around me. I rested my head on his shoulder. He didn't speak until he was certain all nervousness had left me.

"I got a little more information from those pages you gave me," he said. "The ship's position was given and I checked that. Obviously it wasn't too far out when it blew up. I figure it drifted, or maybe even proceeded under its own power until the water overwhelmed it."

"I wonder if Uncle Lew figured something like that must have happened."

"Perhaps," Jeff said. "Especially when he found the remains of the lifeboat. He may even have spoken about it to someone. He may have gone out as you did, searched along the sea bottom and saw the dark shadow down there, but he couldn't dive. Even if he could have, he was too old to do so."

"Then if he did speak of it to someone besides you, his life was in danger from that moment on," I reasoned.

"There's no other answer," Jeff said. "The way I see it now, the stowaways slipped aboard, probably well-armed. They remained hidden until close enough to shore when they let themselves be found. The captain was given orders to put them to work. That much we know. From that point on, we have to go on supposition. I believe they either killed or tied up the crew then the passengers. After that, they forced your father to open the safe. They looted everything of value, then probably killed your father. After that they affixed the explosive and took to the lifeboat.

118

When the ship blew up, that was the end."

"If only it weren't all based on supposition," I said.

"It isn't," Jeff said remindfully. "We found the yacht and we have part of the log, thanks to your daring."

"But no witnesses," I sighed wearily. "I wonder if there's anything on that sunken hulk they want."

"If there is, all they'd have to do is get a diving suit and use it to go down and get whatever they want," Jeff mused. "And if that's the case, why did they have to kill your uncle? And why was your aunt killed?"

I shook my head wearily. "The more I think about it, the more confused I become."

"That's because you're tired," Jeff said. "I'm going to stand guard again tonight, just as I did last night. I'll probably prowl the house so if you hear sounds, don't be frightened. Leave your door ajar as before."

He accompanied me upstairs, again insisting on inspecting my room. As before, I gave him a comforter to wrap himself in, though I knew he'd not likely use it.

His hands enclosed my face and he kissed me tenderly. I bade him good night and closed the door. It was a warm, protected feeling I had knowing I was guarded by the man I loved and who, in turn, loved me.

No sounds in the house would test my nerves tonight. No voice on the wind would send fear shooting through me. No harm would come to me so long as Jeff was nearby.

NINE

The church had been filled with mourners for Aunt Nancy, the soliloquy eloquent, but as I'd walked up the aisle with Jeff at my side, all eyes had been hostile. Yet what had I done to deserve such treatment? In the front pew on the opposite side from the one Jeff and I occupied stood Abner and his sister. His eyes beamed hatred each time he glanced my way. So that was it. He believed I'd caused my aunt's death. That I was her murderess. I wanted to shout out my innocence, yet I knew I could not make a scene. I'd suffered their snubs after the death of my father, then my uncle. I would continue to suffer them until Jeff and I uncovered the reason for all this tragedy.

I felt a numbness all through me as I sat listlessly before the fireplace which Jeff had lit when we entered the house. I had risen that morning to another gray day, the fog having come in during the night. It suited the sad occasion, but did nothing to lift my spirits.

Now Jeff moved about the parlor, lighting lamps, for it was already afternoon. He was still angered by the treatment I'd received. The stubborn set of his jaw gave mute evidence of it.

"Janet, will you please go to New York?" he pleaded for about the fifth time. "I'll stay here until I solve this mystery. The terror you've been through is enough without your having to endure the slight of the entire village."

"I've endured it so long, I can endure it a little longer," I said, my voice a monotone. "I don't think I could without your comforting presence, but with you, I can suffer any slight or accusation they wish to make against me."

He came over to join me on the settee. "You shouldn't

have to put up with such treatment. Perhaps we should call in Silas Bixby after all and tell him about that faceless thing you saw up on the widow's walk."

"My aunt saw it on the veranda first, but she isn't here to substantiate my statement," I said with a sigh. "And after the hostile way Abner Pauley regarded me in church, I know he has spread ugly rumors that I am in some way responsible for her death. Even you don't know I'm speaking the truth."

"Don't say that," he protested, taking me in his arms. "Don't even think it. I love you. I believe in you. I know well what you've been through."

I managed a smile. "Thank you, my beloved."

"Thank you for addressing me so," Jeff said, kissing my brow. "I'm tortured with the fear some harm may come to you."

"Since it's known now in the village you're my only friend, misfortune could well befall you," I argued.

"I don't think so, Janet," he said thoughtfully. "I'm not a part of this."

"You've helped me a great deal," I said.

"No one knows that," he disputed. "I don't believe whoever is behind this considers me a menace, but I'm certain they fear you."

"Darling Jeff," I said, warmed by the love revealed in his eyes, "you've been with me most of the day. I'll not keep you longer."

"I'm not leaving you," he said.

"I'm not frightened," I said. "You made another search of the house after our return. I feel quite safe with the lamps burning and the fireplace crackling."

"There are sufficient logs here to see you through tonight," he said. "Though I expect to return before then. I do wish to send a telegraph to a friend, asking that he dispatch one of those diving suits they use to investigate wrecks."

"How wonderful!" I exclaimed. "Please go at once, my darling. With that, all our questions may be answered."

"If I'm not back by darkness, go to your room and remain there," he cautioned.

"I will," I assured him.

After he left, I wandered aimlessly through the house. I entered my aunt's room with the idea of sorting her possessions. Yet just being in the room brought back the dreadful memory of what had happened to her. I was on my way downstairs when the knocker sounded. I'd been so engrossed in my thoughts I'd not even heard the approach of a carriage.

Though a momentary fear shot through me, I ignored it and moved, with firm step, to the door. I opened it to find Daphne Yates and Roy Lacey standing there. My face beamed in pleasure at sight of them.

"I'm ashamed I didn't get here earlier," Daphne said. "But I was too cowardly to make the drive alone."

"How nice of you to think of me," I said. "Please come inside."

I led them into the parlor, glad the lamps were lit and the fireplace aglow with light and warmth.

"I don't blame you for having all the illumination possible," Roy Lacey said, looking around.

"It was Mr. Cameron's idea," I said.

"I'm so glad you have him for a friend," Daphne said. "I was shocked at the treatment you received from the townspeople."

"It came as no surprise," I said. "I've been accorded such treatment since the death of my father . . . which you undoubtedly heard about."

"We did," Mr. Lacey said. "Jeff told us about it at dinner last night."

"Last night?" I queried.

Daphne gave him a chiding look. "Yes. We were his guests at the Inn. Papa was also with us."

"I didn't know." I remembered that Jeff had been smartly attired last night. Strange how I'd not given it a thought at the time. "I'm sure you enjoyed his company."

"We did, thoroughly," Mr. Lacey said. "Of course, with his bankroll money's no object."

"You must be mistaken," I said. "Jeff is a student at Columbia. He's earning money here in the summer lobstering."

"Gracious," Daphne said in surprise. "There must be a great deal of money in it."

122

"I wouldn't say so," I replied.

"It was a most enjoyable dinner," she went on. "And he's such a gracious host."

"Surprising to know that lobstering doesn't pay off well," Roy said. "That was quite a roll he flashed when he paid the dinner check. Does he come here every summer?"

"You'll have to ask him," I replied. "I know little about him."

"A pity he didn't think to ask you," Daphne said, her disappointment obviously false. "You could have been company for Roy."

"I doubt it would have been a suitable time for me to be seen enjoying myself," I said pointedly.

"I agree," Mr. Lacey replied. "That would be completely different than having an innocent lunch with me."

I was stunned for, though his features bore a look of complete innocence, I knew he was mocking me. I was hurt that Jeff hadn't told me about the dinner. I wondered too why he kept proclaiming his love and concern for me when, at the same time, he sought out Daphne's companionship. I recalled how Nancy had told me about seeing them at the inn. They were still together that night when I ran to the village seeking help. He was with her again last night. Could it be I'd been completely taken in by him? I decided to turn the conversation away from him.

"Please tell me about yourselves," I said. "You first, Daphne."

"I fear there's nothing to tell except I'm a very lazy person," she replied. "I love parties, pretty clothes, gracious homes."

"Then you must be very bored here," I suggested.

"I try not to show it," she said, her smile a simper. "Papa likes me to travel with him. Usually I enjoy it, but then we've never encountered anything like this before."

"Like what?" I asked directly.

"Your poor aunt," she said, her lovely face suddenly assuming a mournful mien. "That's why Roy and I came, really. To once again persuade you to leave this place."

"I wouldn't think of it," I said. "I have a great deal to do. I was just about to go through my aunt's effects when you arrived."

123

Suddenly I wanted these two well-meaning people out of my house. I felt uneasy without knowing why, but I felt they were playing a little game with me. A cat-and-mouse game, though I was probably being unfair.

"In that case, we will go," Daphne said rising.

"I hope you'll forgive me," I said, also rising.

"Certainly," Roy Lacey said, moving with Daphne and me to the door, though he seemed reluctant to go.

I sighed with relief as I bade them farewell and closed the door on them. But as quickly, the silence of the house seemed to close in on me. I was a fool. They'd wanted to remain, but I was too edgy. I went to the kitchen, prepared a light snack and made a pot of tea. I still had no appetite, but the tea served to warm me and lift my spirits.

But, despite the lamps, a gloominess seemed to descend on the house with the coming of darkness and I prayed for Jeff's swift return. I didn't dare open the door to call to him, but I did attempt to pierce the darkness by stepping into the darkened dining room and peering out the window. I was pleased to see the thickness of the fog had dissipated and there were now only patches of it here and there. I supposed it was still heavy though, out on the water, for I could hear the fog horn and its mournful wail. An hour later, when I could no longer hear the sound, I again looked out. I breathed a sigh of relief to see all trace of the fog gone.

Jeff had warned me to seek the protection of my room if he hadn't returned before darkness. Yet I found I was unable to stand even the confinement of the house. I suddenly felt angry and defiant and wanted to confront the person or persons who wished to commit violence upon me. I went upstairs, dressed warmly and went down to the kitchen where I procured a hurricane lantern. Probably what I was about to do was madness, but with the fog clearing, I believed the lights would make an appearance as would the voice calling my name and this time I was going to seek it out.

I got the dory out of the boathouse and into the water. I dropped the anchor, quietly placed the oars in the locks and sat there, ready to move the moment I saw the lights or heard the voice. I kept my eyes on the sea and thought my every sense was alert, I felt all tenseness leave me, for it was peaceful here. The only sound was the lap of the waves.

My thoughts turned to Jeff. I loved him and I wanted to trust him, yet I had a strange element of doubt regarding him, the feeling that, though not lying to me, he was being evasive. I wondered about his interest in Daphne, for he must be as aware of her beauty as I.

Then all thought of him left my mind for I saw the red light appear. It wasn't as visible as when I was in the lookout room and it disappeared from time to time. Obviously, it must be in a boat and was blotted out temporarily as the boat moved with the waves.

Then the voice came. I could easily have left the boat and sought out the dubious protection of the house, but I steeled myself and lifted the anchor. I gripped the oars and set out toward the light. I was cautious, moving the oars through the water as skillfully as possible, for sounds travel easily and well over the water. I hoped to surprise whoever was out there. I forgot my fear in my determination to end this mysttery.

I kept my eye on the poplar tree because the red lights seemed to be just about over the hulk of the yacht. Now and then I looked over my shoulder, but the lights were gone and the voice had ceased. I rowed around the area for half an hour without finding a trace of anything. I seemed to be alone on this vast sweep of ocean. For my part, I'd heard no rattle of oarlocks, no dip of the oars. It seemed to me that there couldn't have been anything human out here.

I could do no more now than row back and with every fall of the oars, my fears increased. I gave one final, sturdy pull at the oars, drove the boat onto the beach near the big rock. I waded ashore and dragged the dory after me. To my everlasting amazement, I saw another boat hauled up and tied. Even from a distance, I knew it was Jeff's. I went over to it, found the oars dripping. That boat had just put in. If there'd been a boat out there where the red lights and the voice originated, it could very well have been this one.

I hurried up the slope, carrying the lighted lantern, because it didn't matter if I was seen. As I walked close by the trees and shrubs serving as a windbreak for the house, Jeff stepped out.

"Janet, what are you doing down at the beach?" he asked.

"How long have you been here?" I countered his question with another.

"Only a few minutes. I'm always saying how sorry I am for being delayed, but it was unavoidable."

"I saw your boat. You must have put in while I was out rowing around hunting for the source of the red light and the voice. Did you see or hear it?"

"No. Did you find anything?"

"Nothing. It's possible I was seen launching my boat by whoever was out there. The lights and the voices stopped as I started out."

"You shouldn't have gone alone," he chided me. "It could be very dangerous."

"I had to do something. I suddenly felt angry at whoever is doing this to me, so I came down here to wait for the lights and the voice. When they came, I lost all of my fears somehow. I'm much more scared now thinking about it than I was out there looking for it. Did you get off your message?"

"Yes, and there was a telegram waiting. A further report on sinkings here. There were no ships reported missing about the time your father's yacht vanished, and no reports of any sinkings off the bluff in more than fifty years. The ship down there is the yacht all right."

"I'm sure of it now," I said, wondering why that small errand had taken all afternoon and half the night.

I blew out the lantern after we reached the porch. Our rockers made pleasant little squeaks as we sat in silence for a few moments while I got back my breath.

"How soon will the diving suit arrive?" I asked hopefully.

"It's being brought by a special messenger," Jeff replied. "At least a day or two. I know that probably seems like an eternity. That's why I'd be better pleased if you'd go to New York. Leave this to me. I can handle it alone."

"Have you enlisted the help of Michael Yates and Roy Lacey?" I asked.

"Certainly not," he exclaimed. "What makes you say such a thing?"

"Daphne and Mr. Lacey were here after you left," I informed Jeff. "You've been seeing quite a lot of her, haven't you?"

"Jealous?" he asked, his smile teasing.

"Not a bit," I said stiffly.

He laughed. "Don't be. Yes, I've been seeing them. I'm as curious about them as you."

"How do you know I am?" I asked.

"Because you're intelligent and I'm sure you believe their appearance in the village is more than coincidental."

"True," I admitted. "I felt this afternoon as if they were trying to find out something. I fear I was a little rude in dismissing them."

"I forgive you," he said in that bantering tone.

"I understand you flashed quite a roll of bills," I said.

"So they noticed," Jeff said.

"They were also seeking out information about you," I remarked.

"Good," Jeff said. "That shows they're worried."

"You believe they're implicated?"

"I do. As for the roll of bills, the two or three on the outside were tens, the rest ones. It's known as a Philadelphia roll."

"Jeff, won't it cost a lot of money to rent one of those diving suits?"

"Yes," he admitted. "But I feel the cause is worth any expense."

"I'll pay for it," I said.

"No need to," he replied.

"I'm very curious about you," I said.

"I know," he replied. "Just trust me. And now, you need rest. So let me check your room and after that I'll go through the house."

I sighed, knowing it was useless to question him further. He had a clever way of parrying anything I asked.

TEN

I awoke refreshed, for I'd drifted off to sleep, secure in the feeling Jeff would allow no harm to come to me. He left a note on the kitchen table, informing me that he'd breakfasted here and coffee was on the back of the stove, still warm. He added further assurance that another search of the house revealed all was well.

I knew the diving suit would scarcely arrive today and I felt I couldn't wait, despite Jeff's warning I not go out there alone. I'd have far preferred he be with me, but I didn't know when or if he would come. Also, while it would be wiser to go when the sun was high and could pierce the murky bottom, there was no sun. The day was bleak and it could well be the fog would once again make its relentless way to shore. If I was going to dive, I must do so now.

I went to the boathouse, changed to my bathing suit. Fortunately there was still a goodly supply of large stones in the dory. Before I was ten minutes from shore, the wind began whipping my face. I looked around and saw the fog bank, still miles out, but drifting in slowly, relentlessly. I was glad I'd started now. I estimated that the fog, with the help of the wind, would reach the area of the sunken yacht in about an hour and a half. That gave me time enough to reach the spot, make my dive, and investigate the contents of the ship's safe again. If the jewelry was there, I wanted to get it before the thieves did. I would return it to the rightful heirs of those unfortunate passengers who had died with Papa when the yacht went down. I wanted, more than anything, to vindicate Papa's name.

I reached the spot, lifted the oars and drifted about for

a few moments searching for the lobster trap below the surface. When I found it, I dropped anchor and stood up, ready to dive. There wasn't a moment to waste. The fog bank, like a wall of solid substance, was moving relentlessly. I'd have to complete my dive and then begin rowing back, perhaps through the advance mists. If I was caught in the main fog bank, I could easily get lost and find myself in a serious predicament.

Jeff was right. I should not attempt these dives alone. However I felt that this could not wait. I knew my capabilities as well as I knew the fog. To me the risk was not as great as Jeff indicated it could be.

I grasped two of the stones, dove overside and the stones helped carry me down. In seconds, I reached the now-familiar shape of the sunken yacht and, without hesitation, I clawed my way through the opening in her hull and reached the safe again. I doubted that if it contained a strong box—as they all did for storing the valuables of passengers—it would have fallen out of the safe, for the sea had been very calm since I discovered the safe. I felt with both hands inside the steel compartment. There was nothing. The safe had been looted of all but that log book, which they'd probably not thought worth the taking.

My lungs were beginning to ache. It was time to go up. The water was murky because of the lack of sun, but as I began to swim out of the aperture I floundered about to clear myself and my hands came into contact with a slender, hard substance. Some of it broke loose and floated before my astonished eyes. I had blundered into a skeleton.

If it had been possible to scream under water, I would have done so. Nothing had upset me as much as this. I kicked at the wreck to force myself to the surface and it seemed to take hours in my near panic. My lungs were bursting when I bobbed up and I opened my mouth and sucked in all the air my lungs could hold.

I kept thinking of that skeleton. It could even have been the remains of Papa. The water suddenly felt deathly cold. I flipped over on my back to rest. My dory was fifty feet away, but I didn't feel I had the strength to swim to it for another two or three minutes. If I hadn't seen that skeleton, I'd have been all right, but the sight of it sapped my stamina.

The reason for the chill was apparent because, as I watched the dory, the advance elements of the fog bank began to close in around it. That stirred me to action and removed some of my exhaustion. I turned over and began to swim.

I'd taken not half a dozen strokes before something seized my ankle and pulled me under. It happened so fast that I didn't even have time to draw in the air I needed and almost at once I felt the lack of oxygen acutely. All I could think of in my wild fright was that the skeleton, which had disassembled as I touched it, was now pulling me under. My right leg was free. I jerked it up, kicked back and the heel came hard against what seemed to be a jaw. I was promptly released. I rose to the surface and breathed. Now the fog had closed in. The wind must have grown even stronger to move that mass so quickly.

There was someone swimming close by me. Had I been able to turn on my back, I might have seen who it was, but this man had tried to keep me under once and obviously intended to finish his grisly task if he could seize me again. So my salvation lay in swimming fast. Into the fog, preferably, where he couldn't find me. I was sure I'd be able to locate the dory.

A dim form came alongside me. I saw a hand reach out. I kicked my heels and went into a dive. I swam under water, surfaced, and there were no signs of this would-be murderer.

I was orienting myself to head for the dory when I had another glimpse of him. He was swimming strongly in my direction. I was able to see that his bathing suit was a dark blue. Like Jeff's, it occurred to me, but I had no time to dwell upon that. I dived again, avoided him and struck out hard in the direction I hoped the dory would be. If I found it and got aboard, I might be able to locate the swimmer and discover just who he was.

I heard a man's voice call out. I couldn't recognize it for the thickening fog distorted it too much, but it was followed by the creak of oarlocks. If the murderer had found my dory and was escaping in it, I might be finished. I was still strong enough to swim ashore if I didn't lose my way and that was a problem where my chance would be none too good. The fog was growing heavier minute by minute. When the main bank hit, everything would be completely obscured. I began to fear I'd not get out of this.

Suddenly, out of the fog, the prow of a boat loomed up. Someone aboard shouted, "There she is!"

They were going to run me down or get close enough to hit me with an oar. My tired heart was beating faster than ever, my lungs ached from all the diving I'd had to do, but there was no help for it. I waited until I heard the dip of the oars close by before I dived. I swam as long and as far as I possibly could before coming up.

I turned on my back, gasping for air. When the gasps subsided enough, I listened for the sound of the oars, but didn't hear them. Without question, whoever was in that boat was heading for shore by now, inspired by the ever-growing density of the fog.

I rested only as long as I dared and then struck out. Ashore, the fog horn began its chant and it guided me in the right direction. I floundered around for ten minutes before I found the dory, but there it was, sound and secure. I clambered aboard and simply lay there for a time. I didn't know how long. In my weakness, and in the chill fog,, I felt utter defeat, though I'd accomplished my purpose and saved my life.

Finally I sat up and began rowing. I knew how to follow the wail of the horn. It had saved many a ship in its long existence and now it was saving my life. Without it, I'd likely have circled until I grew too tired to row and then turn adrift to whatever fate the fog and the sea had for me.

By the time my boat beached, the fog was so thick I didn't even know what section of the beach I'd arrived at. I jumped into the water, pulled the boat to a safe place, tied it to a large rock and then I took stock of my location. I thought I was about a quarter of a mile south of the rock, where the slope off the bluff ended.

I walked in that direction. At times I think I staggered out of weariness, but I came to the rock and I blessed it a dozen times. I kept on going. To stop now would relax my tired muscles so I'd not get started again quickly enough, and the cold fog pressed in on my soaking wet bathing suit.

I climbed the path to the house. In my room, I got out of my wet suit, toweled myself briskly and dressed. Then I went to the kitchen where I made a pot of tea. I brought it into the parlor, along with a cup and saucer. I touched a match to papers and fresh kindling which Jeff had seen fit to build in the fireplace before he left. I sat there rocking and sipping tea and telling myself I was safe. That it would be stupid to give in to the hysterics which had been threatening me ever since my encounter with the remains of the skeleton and that murderous swimmer. I tried to think straight, to determine in my mind who that man was. The suit was like Jeff's, but it resembled the type all men used.

At least I knew that, whoever my enemies were, they were aware of the location of the sunken yacht. I'd learned there was no jewelry in the safe, but it could well be in some other part of the ship. I breathed a prayer that the diving suit would arrive tomorrow and that there would be no fog.

I was so engrossed in my thoughts that the sound of the door knocker startled me. Thinking it might be Jeff, I walked with quickened step, but it was only Roy Lacey.

"May I come in, Miss Vance?" he asked. "I'm here on an urgent matter."

I stepped aside, motioning for him to enter, leading him back to the parlor. He moved over to the welcoming heat of the fireplace.

"It's about the house," he began at once. "Mr. Yates has agreed to offer you fifty thousand dollars. But you must accept immediately as he wishes work begun at once."

"I thought I'd made myself clear on that subject," I said.

"That was before your aunt's death," he said.

"I haven't changed my opinion," I said firmly.

"But how can you wish to continue living here?"" he asked. "Ignored by all in the village?"

"I don't concern myself with them," I said.

"My dear, in time you will beome embittered. Please," he pleaded, "I beg of you, give it serious thought."

I was truly impressed with the figure, yet I was more determined than ever to remain. "Mr. Lacey, I won't deny your arguments might, in time, sway me, but at the present time, I'm still too affected by the death of my aunt."

"I know, but I must bring back an answer today. You do think the offer fair, don't you?"

"A more than generous one," I agreed. "But my answer is no."

"A pity," he said, shaking his head. "Mr. Yates will be sorely disappointed as will be his daughter. She is most anxious to leave this dreary spot. She said as much to Jeff this afternoon."

"You mean Mr. Cameron is with her?" I asked, unable to conceal my surprise.

"I hope," he said, in feigned embarrassment, "I didn't say anything I shouldn't."

"No," I replied smiling. "Why shouldn't he seek the company of a beautiful girl? After all, he's a very handsome young man."

"They make a handsome couple, and I daresay Daphne has her eye on him."

"I wish her success," I said, my smile as false as his.

"I'm sorry to have to carry back such bad news," Mr. Lacey said. "You will excuse me. The fog is too bad to delay my return."

I saw him to the door, watching the fog close in behind his carriage. The tears I'd fought threatened to come. Not because of fear, but because of despair. How could I continue to believe in Jeff when he still sought out the company of Daphne? Could it be he was involved in a conspiracy with them? Was there no one I could turn to? As quickly, the answer came. No one but myself. If that was the way it had to be, I would do my best.

An hour later, a messenger came from the village with a note from Mr. Yates. He suggested I think over his offer for another twenty-four hours. He'd be in the village that long. Perhaps I would accept, I thought dismally. But perhaps I could learn a lot more in twenty-four hours.

Jeff made no appearance up until the hour of ten o'clock when I retired. I pushed a chest against my door and left my lamp turned low. I heard no sounds, there was no doleful voice calling my name and no lights, thanks to the fog. Despite my loneliness, I drifted off into blessed sleep, not awakening until eight the following morning.

ELEVEN

I spent the day in my aunt's room, sorting out her possessions. I wrote a letter to Mr. LeMay Fillmore, who had been my uncle's attorney, informing him of my aunt's tragic death. I told him, in detail, of all that had happened and asked for his help. I would need an attorney now. Perhaps in him I would also have a friend.

My spirits lifted when the sun broke through in late afternoon. I'd determined to go out on the water again tonight if the fog dissipated. I was going to learn who was calling my name. Though the voice sounded ghostly, I believed it to be human.

I thought of Jeff and suddenly felt a growing concern. He'd been my only ally and it wasn't like him to remain away. Suppose he was ill or had met with foul play. Thinking about him made my fear greater. Impulsively, I went down to the beach, found my dory where I left it and rowed it to Jeff's shack. Though his lobster boat was not there, I went to the shack and knocked anyway. There was no response. I peered through the windows, but everything was neat and orderly. The door was unlocked and I opened it.

I had a clear view of the room. The door of the clothes closet was ajar and I could see something that resembled a human body standing inside. I hastily flung the door wide and went to the closet. I was stunned to find myself staring at something I'd never seen before, but which I recognized from descriptions in newspapers and magazines. I was looking at a diving suit with helmet, a belt of weights, and an air hose.

Jeff had received prompt service in obtaining this, but

he hadn't even come to tell me about it. I doubted he'd been able to use the device with all the fog, but knowing he had it would have encouraged me greatly. I noted one other fact: also in the closet were some of Jeff's clothes. It required only a glance to see that they were made by expensive and fine tailors. The cost of these would be far more than a student, earning his college expenses by working as a lobsterman, could possibly afford.

I rowed back, beached the dory and walked slowly up the slope and over the bluff to the house. I went inside, hopeful there might be a note from Jeff thrust beneath the door. There was nothing. I ate my solitary supper while dusk and then darkness closed in around me, bringing back all the fears and terrors of the night.

I knew well the danger I faced, but I was determined to go. I donned a bathing suit and used a long cape for protection against the night chill. I took along a storm lantern and I left lamps burning in the house to give a visible token that I must be there. I slipped out the back door and hurried down to the beach.

Once again I lined up the boat with the lone poplar on the bluff. I rowed out quickly, pausing now and then with the oars raised, to listen. When I heard no sound, I resumed rowing. There was little use in trying to find the marker over the sunken yacht at night, but I could judge with a reasonable degree of accuracy where it was. I rowed further out, perhaps a quarter of a mile. There I shipped the oars and sat huddled on the bottom of the boat.

I had no idea how much time elapsed. I guessed it must have been two long, lonely hours, filled with nothing but apprehension and a growing sense of loneliness. I told myself I was a fool for coming out here alone. No matter who or what appeared to cause the voice and lights, how could I cope with it? Twice I almost gave in to the urge to row ashore at once and get out of that house. Reason prevailed only with considerable effort on my part, backed by the knowledge that I was here to clear the name of my father and, if possible, solve the mystery of the deaths of my aunt and uncle.

I heard the creak of the oarlocks first. They were faint,

but growing louder, finally coordinating with the dip and splash of the oars themselves. Then the sounds died abruptly and, for a few moments, I heard nothing. It was too dark to see what was close by me, but that same darkness concealed me. Then I saw the flare of a match, after which the red lights appeared. There were three of them, moving slightly in the breeze, indicating they must be hanging from some sort of line. I heard the voice calling my name. At this close range, there was nothing ghostly about it, though it did have some elusive quality I couldn't place, some echoing effect.

Over and over again, I heard my name called. Back in the house, the effect would be ghostly and terrifying. I quietly plied the oars, swinging the boat about to point it at the source of the voice.

I rowed without haste, raising and lowering the oars in a manner calculated to make a minimum of sound. Suddenly the voice stopped and the red lights went out. I'd been either heard or seen. I now put some strength into my rowing, without bothering to conceal the sounds of my approach. I paused to light the storm lantern at my feet.

A dark shape slid by me. I used one oar to turn swiftly and follow. The craft was just ahead. Whoever was in it seemed to be more confused about my location than I was about his. I dug the oars deeper, bent to them with a will and the light dory closed the distance. I lifted the lantern, held it high. For a few seconds I saw the deathly pale face of Abner Pauley. He was frantically trying to turn his boat.

I saw all I wanted to. Now I had to reach shore before Abner. I rowed as hard as I could, but I sensed that I was no match for him, and I could tell by the sounds that he was gaining on me. If he caught up, he'd try to turn the dory over and then attack me while I was swimming. Once in the water I'd be easy prey for him.

I could barely see the poplar tree and, judging by it, I tried to estimate the distance to shore. I slipped off the cape, kicked off my shoes, lifted the storm lantern to one of the seats. I went overside quietly, gave the dory a hard shove and sent it back out to sea. Then I struck for shore.

Now and then I turned on my back to float and look in

137

the direction of the lantern-lit dory. It was moving and, as I didn't hear any sound of Abner Pauley's boat, I was sure he was still following the dory in the belief I was in it.

Of course, in moments he'd catch up with it and realize he'd been tricked. Then he'd head for shore and begin searching for me. His boat came dangerously close at times as he swept back and forth trying to find me. I waded ashore, dashed down the beach, ran up the slope and across the bluff to the rear of the house. I locked the back door, ran through the well-lighted house to my room where I hastily toweled myself and dressed. I didn't know what to do and I prayed that Jeff would come. I didn't dare leave the house in an attempt to reach the village.

I heard the sound of an approaching carriage and my heart quickened its already wild beat. I went downstairs, comforted only by the many lamps burning. The knocker sounded and I asked who it was.

Daphne Yates identified herself. I slid the bolt, but opened the door only inches. I noticed two carriages outside, yet she was alone.

"What is it, Daphne?"

"Aren't you going to ask me in?" she asked. She was carrying a portmanteau. "You shouldn't be alone in this house. I came to spend the night with you."

"I don't believe you."

She looked so startled at my words that I knew I'd spoken the truth. I slammed the door, shot the bolt and leaned wearily against the door. A moan of despair escaped me.

"I suppose it is discouraging to learn your efforts to outwit us have failed." The voice came from behind me. It was that of Michael Yates. I stiffened in fear. "I admire your courage, your spirit and your faith in your father's innocence," he continued. "But you've failed in your quest."

I turned around slowly. There was no escape for me. I was flanked by Abner Pauley, Michael Yates and Roy Lacey. Outside, I heard one of the carriages pull away. That would be Daphne. I knew then they were going to murder me. I'd go over the cliff as my uncle had before me. I made up my mind in that moment that if I did, I'd do so only in an attempt to escape them. I'd fight. I was certain my father had, in an effort to protect his passengers and crew.

"What do you want of me?" I asked in my anguish.

"We're not going to harm you," Michael Yates said smoothly.

"A pity you have such an insatiable curiosity," Lacey said smoothly. "You're much too young and beautiful to die."

"Shut up, Roy," Yates said.

"How did you get in here?" My hands had slid up behind me to the bolt and were slowly pushing it back.

Abner held up two keys. "I stole them from a hook in the pantry the night of your uncle's accidental death. I had come here to console your aunt."

"You killed her," my voice was contemptuous. "She trusted you."

Michael Yates said, "Most unfortunate. Roy had been in the cellar all that day. Nancy came to tell Abner about the log. I already knew about it, having seen you dive for it and bring it back. It was Roy who stole it from the widow's walk."

"And left a corroded button there to make me think it was my father who had come to reclaim it," I said bitterly.

"A very good touch, I thought," Roy said, looking pleased with himself. "I found them in the cellar. I spent a lot of time there until Jeff Cameron started guarding the place."

"Which of you killed my aunt?" I asked.

"That really was an accident," Michael Yates said. "It was I who was dressed in the captain's uniform, my face concealed by a scarf. In the fog it appeared I had no face. Abner and I entered the house when you went outside. He lured Nancy from her room and brought her up there, knowing she was superstitious. She'd already seen me on the veranda where I'd attracted her attention by walking back and forth. The fog helped create the illusion I was faceless and I thought the seaweed a good touch. When she saw me again on the widow's walk, she lost her footing on the ladder and fell. Since she was dead, Roy placed another button in her hand in the hope you'd really believe it was your father haunting the place."

"What is it you're after?" I asked wearily.

"The missing pages from the log." Michael Yates answered my question. "I searched the house while you lunched with Roy, but could find no trace of them."

"I don't have them," I said.

The bolt was slipped and I was ready to make my dash for freedom when one of the horses outside whinnied.

"Abner, go up to the lookout," Yates commanded. "See if the pages to the log are in the desk. Roy, go out the back door and watch out for Cameron. Use your gun if you have to. I'm going to persuade Janet to give up those pages."

"I don't have them," I cried out, knowing he meant to use force on me.

Abner had already gone upstairs. Roy started toward the kitchen. This was my last chance. I turned the knob, opened the door and tried to slip through, but Yates was prepared for me.

He reached out, grabbed my wrist and flung me toward the parlor. I was caught off balance and fell. Yates picked up a lamp, threw it against the lighted fireplace. It smashed and flaming oil splashed on the rug, igniting it. A tablecloth caught fire as did a drapery and lace curtain. The room seemed alive with fire.

Yates bent over and dragged me to my feet. He pulled and dragged me to the door. When I started to strike at him, he forced my hands behind my back, holding my wrists at an angle that made pain shoot up my arm. I couldn't struggle in such a position and he pushed me ahead of him. I knew we were heading for the cliff. The outside was well lighted, for the parlor was completely aflame and I knew the fire would quickly spread to the rest of the house, for the open front door created a strong draft.

"Janet, Janet!" My name was being called, but this time there was an edge of terror to it. It was Jeff and he obviously had seen the flames. But for me, I knew it was too late. I was to meet the same fate as my uncle.

"Go back, Jeff," I cried. "Go back. Roy Lacey has a gun."

But I was too late, for I heard the sharp retort of the weapon as it was fired. Then I heard running footsteps. I moaned, for it had to be Lacey. Jeff had walked into a trap and been killed. A surge of anger coursed through me and I suddenly stopped, catching Yates off balance. I kicked back with my heel. He howled as I connected with his leg bone.

I struggled, miraculously freed myself and ran in a parallel direction with the cliff.

"Janet, get down . . . drop to the ground!" It was Jeff's voice! I fell rather than dropped, for I'd reached the limit of my endurance, both physically and mentally.

I saw Jeff flash past me as he pursued Yates. I didn't know where Lacey was, nor did I care, so long as he didn't get to me. I heard a wild cry, a piercing scream, then silence. I didn't know if it was Jeff or Yates, but I had a mental picture of a body hurtling into space and crashing to the rocks below. The thought of such a fate happening to Jeff sent a shock of terror through me and merciful unconsciousness embraced me.

I awoke in a strange bed in a strange room. I looked up and saw Jeff sitting at the side of the bed. My hand was enclosed in his.

"You're in a room at the village," he said softly. "You've been through a lot, my darling, but it's over now. The mystery is ended."

Slowly, memory returned and, without speaking, my eyes asked what had happened after I fainted.

"Roy Yates tried to kill me as I came up the path," Jeff said. "We struggled for the gun and it went off. He isn't badly injured, but a bullet in the thigh will give him plenty of time to tell the constable what he and his partner were up to. As for Michael Yates, in trying to escape from me, he went over the cliff. Poetic justice of a sort, I guess."

"Was Daphne in on the scheme?" I asked.

"Yes," he said. "She's talking to the constable now."

"Abner Pauley?" I asked.

"You know the house burned down," he said.

I nodded. I knew then Abner was consumed in the flames. He couldn't possibly have escaped.

"They paid for their crime," I said, wondering why I felt so weak.

"You mustn't talk," Jeff said. "The doctor wishes to give you a sedative. When the story comes out, everyone in the village will beg your forgiveness."

That didn't seem important now. "What about Daphne?"

"She's making arrangements to have her father's body shipped back to New York."

"I mean . . . you and Daphne."

"Darling," he said softly, "I love only you. I sought out her company in an attempt to learn why she and her father and so-called secretary were here. She, in turn, was doing her utmost to keep me away from you. She almost succeeded. She asked me to meet her at the inn. When I got there, neither she, her father nor Lacey were there. I suspected and got back as fast as possible. I almost didn't get here in time. You must rest. The doctor's outside."

"Don't leave me," I said, frightened.

"Only long enough to summon him," Jeff said, bending over me, kissing me gently, but with all his love. "One thing more—my real name is Jeff Plant. It was my father and mother who owned the *Cecelia*. When I read of your uncle's accidental death, I came here at once. It struck me as a little too odd. No more talking now, my darling."

A year has passed since that awful night and what happened on that ship is now known to the public. It was Michael Yates who sent that infamous wireless befouling Papa's good name. The murderer of my aunt and uncle paid with his life. Roy Lacey made a complete confession, and paid dearly for what he helped to do to the passengers on the *Cecelia*. As for Daphne, I asked for leniency in her case. She'd really done me no harm and she would have to live with the knowledge of the awful crime her father committed for the rest of her life.

For it was Michael Yates and Roy Lacey who were the stowaways aboard the yacht. They murdered my father after he opened the safe. He'd been assured by them that they'd not harm the crew or passengers if he did so. It was done late at night while all aboard were sleeping. They'd also murdered two crew members who were about.

They took the jewels with them in the lifeboat after planting explosives on the yacht. They partially burned and buried the lifeboat. When I discovered it, they took it elsewhere. In the village, they made Abner's acquaintance, quickly became aware of his greed. They paid him to bring them any information regarding the sinking of the *Cecelia*. When Uncle Lew went to Abner to have him order a diving suit, Abner immediately sent word to Yates and Lacey. Abner also informed them of my uncle's suspicions.

They came to the village, sought the proper opportunity and did my uncle in. They couldn't allow anyone to discover the wreck, for the fact that the ladies had brought their jewels to wear and display for the occasion of their voyage was well known. They should still be on the wreck and if its whereabouts was known, their heirs could well afford to hire divers to go down for them. If that happened, the hole in the side would be discovered, foul play would be suspected and an investigation begun.

With the death of my uncle, all would have been fine, for just at that time, they had found buyers for their stolen loot. However, when I spread word I didn't believe my uncle's death accidental, I presented an added menace to them and they had to do away with me. When I found the log, the peril became even greater. Not only were they in danger of being found out, but all their efforts would be for naught, for no one would want the jewelry.

Abner Pauley perished in the fire. His greed proved his undoing. He'd been promised a share in the profits, but somehow, I believe he'd have eventually met the same fate as my uncle.

It was Michael Yates's idea to burn the house down. He was the brain behind the entire scheme. I posthumously would have been accused of the death of my uncle and aunt to acquire their estate, but my conscience would haunt me so that my sanity became affected. I burned down the house and took my life by jumping over the cliff.

It was quite a scheme and almost succeeded except for Jeff's quick intervention.

We're happily married now and settled in New York. I have no desire to ever return to the village where I knew such mental agony. However, before I left the townsfolk showed their true spirit by giving a memorial service in the church for both Papa and Uncle Lew. The gesture warmed my heart. I knew it was all my Uncle Lew ever wanted ... vindication for Papa.

I still love the sea. I love the sound of the pounding surf, the cries of the gulls as they swoop over it. I no longer feel fear when I see lights on the water, for they're not there to frighten me. And yet, when I hear a voice drift on the wind across the water, I shudder in memory of the one that called to me. But then I remind myself all that is over and my life now is filled with love and good cheer.

As for the jewels, Lacey turned them over before his trial for murder on the high seas, and they were given to the rightful heirs.